COOKING WITH THE DOC

JENNIFER YOUNGBLOOD
CRAIG DEPEW, MD

DITCH LILY PRESS

YOUR FREE BOOK AWAITS

Get Beastly Charm: A Contemporary retelling of beauty & the beast as a welcome gift when you sign up for my newsletter. You'll get information on my new releases, book recommendations, discounts, and other freebies.

Get the book at:

http://bit.ly/freebookjenniferyoungblood

PROLOGUE

It was controlled chaos in the operating room. Dr. Samuel Wallentine said a silent prayer, thanking God for the air conditioning that protected them from the brutal Afghan summer sun. He labored in the Army's most advanced field hospital. It consisted of a fully equipped, four-bed operating room packaged inside a steel shipping container. These units could be put on a trailer or slung under a helicopter. The Army had plopped four of them side by side on top of a plateau at Forward Operating Base Belleview. His job was to tie off bleeding vessels, place organs back where they belonged, and prepare wounded soldiers for medevac to a much larger Stage C hospital.

Sam was proud of the work they did at Combat Support Hospital. Because they managed to keep so many men and women alive through the *golden hour* after they were wounded, many more survived than would have otherwise. Many more families still had daddies and mommies, brothers and sisters, daughters and sons at the dinner table instead of beneath heroic tombstones.

First Sergeant Mirabelle Walker the RN running their outfit strolled among the four operating tables. Sam thought she was probably the cutest soldier in the Army, and he enjoyed having her around. She was just the right combination of flirty, professional and lethal.

Even though she was five foot three inches tall, Sam was pretty sure she could take down any Taliban terrorist with one hand tied behind her back. During downtime she was the friendly little sister anyone would want, but when there was work to be done, she was all business.

At Table Alpha the team sat and chatted. "I don't care what Andreotti says. There's no way Milan can beat Madrid for the World Cup."

"I remember the good old days, when soldiers just argued about American football," Mirabelle interrupted. "Stick a bunch of good men overseas, and all of a sudden, they're experts on world sports."

"You know what they say, 'When in Rome…'"

"Yeah, and when in Kabul, kick around a goat's head like the locals do?" She made a face. "I don't think so," she retorted. The men laughed and went back to their argument.

At the other end of the OR, surgical teams were finishing up their last two cases of the morning on Table Charlie and Table Delta. Outside, a Blackhawk helicopter beat a steady rhythm while its engines idled, waiting to whisk the patients away and make room for more wounded. Techs were standing by to sanitize the tables as soon as the cases were finished and carried out the back door to the choppers.

Mirabelle stopped at Table Bravo, where Sam sat on a metal folding chair reading a journal article about septic shock on the battlefield. He set it down and smiled at her. "Hey there, Mirabelle."

"Hiya, doc," she replied. She didn't use her military voice but spoke to him in sweet, sing-song tones. "Don't you already know enough? Whatcha learning?"

He picked up the surgical journal and pointed to the headline of the article. "This guy claims that bullet and IED wounds can get infected. Gee, who'd have guessed?"

"Better make sure and wear your gloves," she quipped. "You know, I ordered those special just for your ginormous hands."

A grin tugged at his lips. "I kinda figured that," he drawled. "Too bad nobody else gets this color." He picked a glove out of the box attached to the wall. Everyone in the OR wore lilac-colored nitrile gloves for non-sterile work. Everyone, that was, except Sam. His were pink ... an obnoxious, bright, hot pink. "Do they glow in the dark too?" he teased.

Her eyes sparkled with an eager glow. "I don't know. Let's hang out after our shift, and we can find out."

He shook his head, tsking his tongue. "Now, Mirabelle, what would your boyfriend think if he heard you say that?"

The corners of her mouth pulled down. "I don't have a boyfriend. You'd think that here, surrounded by dozens of big, burly soldiers and Marines, I could find one but nope."

Mirabelle was fun to banter with. "There's that huge, scary Special Forces guy I saw winking at you."

Pink tinged her cheeks, her hands going to her hips. "Dave's not scary. He's just a big teddy bear."

"Yeah, well I'm terrified of him," Sam said dryly.

A klaxon sounded outside. Immediately, Sergeant Mirabelle got serious, putting her hand to her earpiece. She nodded and mumbled something into her microphone. Raising her head, she called out to her crew. "Listen up people. Casualties arriving in five minutes. IED ambush on a humanitarian convoy. We're expecting at least eight victims."

Sam put a surgery cap over his brown, military-cut hair and tied on his mask. He scrubbed in, and a medic helped him into his sterile gown. The medic had to stand on a footstool to reach around his broad shoulders. His green eyes were all that showed between his mask and cap. He had his personal supply of sterile gloves, since no one else wore size eight and a half. They weren't pink though. All of the sterile gloves were bland tan-colored. He grinned a little thinking of the pink.

Sam was ten hours into a twelve-hour shift. He shook the ache out of his shoulders and the fatigue from his back and brain. The team members were allowed to get out of the surgical unit and take in some fresh air between cases, but for the most part, they didn't bother. It was sweltering outside, and the sun was so blazing that it was worse than staying inside. Besides, the air outside tended to be contaminated with sniper's bullets zipping in from the surrounding hills. That absolutely made it more pleasant inside the bulletproof container. The medic finished putting Sam's gown on him and slapped him on both shoulders. "Hang in there, doc. Two more hours. You can do this."

"For God and country," he replied. "Hoorah." Alisha was a Marine, so he could get away with saying that to her.

"Hoorah, sir." Alisha wore a surgical mask to keep his gown sterile, but her eyes smiled at him.

Sam appreciated Alisha's pleasant nature, especially here amidst the gloom of life and death situations where the future turned on a dime. "I'm going to miss working with you when you rotate home this weekend. It's been good."

Her smile widened. "Yeah, but all good deployments end sometime," she said in a practical tone. "These four months have been something else. I can't wait to get home to my husband and kids."

An unexpected pang went through Sam, reminding him that he had no one to go home to. "How many are there? I know you've told me before."

"Three of them. My oldest is eight, a girl. I have two boys—a four-year-old and two-year-old. Oh, and one husband who's the biggest kid of all," she added with a chuckle.

"Get home to them, girl. You don't need to be here anymore."

"That's for sure."

It wasn't easy to keep a positive attitude in circumstances like these. So many good men and women, all of them volunteers, came here to provide safety and freedom for complete strangers. Then not one of those strangers said, "Thanks" or showed much appreciation. The reward for selflessly giving months or years out of their lives was to be spit on, distrusted, and blown up. Sam had seen so much misery and death inflicted upon his countrymen.

Even worse was what these insurgents did to each other. Sam had treated hundreds of local women and children in his time here. In the best cases they'd been ignored and starved. In the worst cases, well, he couldn't focus on the worst ones. To survive here, soldiers had to learn to compartmentalize their experiences. His mental shoeboxes where he stored memories were labeled *Good Times* and *All Other*. Unfortunately, the latter overflowed while the *Good Times* box languished.

Military vehicles rumbled to a stop outside the container. The hospital doors opened and field medics carried in two badly burned and mangled men. "All the way to the end," Mirabelle directed, pointing to the recently cleaned operating tables where the teams had changed into fresh gowns and were standing by. Sam waited his turn.

Two more medics brought a man through the door on a canvas stretcher. Their uniforms were dark green, Afghan army style, not the desert camo of American soldiers. Afghan allies were welcome in the US hospitals, as were civilians and even enemies. Americans served and saved all comers. Mirabelle pointed with her pen. "Bed bravo," she said, indicating Sam's table. The wounded man wore a British uniform soaked in blood, a bullet wound above his left eye. Sam knew he didn't have much to offer the poor boy.

The Afghan soldiers walked out and Sam's team got to work. They cut away the uniform only to discover his Osprey body armor. It was similar to the US armor they were familiar with but different enough that it took a few extra seconds to figure out where the Brits had placed the hooks, snaps, buttons and belts, so the team could remove his ceramic plates.

Sam glanced up. The Afghan medics were back, this time with one of their own wounded. "Bed Alpha," Mirabelle ordered. They placed the man on the table and quickly left.

Sam and his team focused intensely. The anesthetist connected the blood pressure monitor. "No pulse, no BP," he intoned.

"Can't get fluids running. His veins are already clotted," added a medic, his voice hopeless.

Sam studied the man's abdominal wound. The blood was already dry. Not just clotted but really dry, hard, flaky. He reached into the wound. The body was completely cold. This man hadn't been a casualty just this morning. He'd been dead a couple of days already. Why had the Afghans bothered bringing him in? He should have gone straight to the morgue. They'd held onto his body and brought him in with their own guy. Why? The American sentries who guarded the entrance to the base stopped and searched all Afghans who tried to enter. But if they were transporting a coalition casualty, that would have gotten them in on the fast track through the gate and into the base hospital. Besides, these Afghans were friendly. They weren't enemies.

He glanced over at Table Alpha. The team there worked on a flesh wound in the Afghan soldier's left triceps. Not a big deal. He'd be patched up and sent back to his unit to recover. The man smiled at Sam. He raised his head and spoke in English, loud enough for Sam to hear. "Allah is great, my friend. I'm going to Paradise today. I'm taking all of you with me." A red fabric strap dangled from his shirt tail. How curious. It wasn't part of his uniform or his underclothing. In a gut-wrenching punch that nearly stole Sam's breath, he realized what was happening.

Sam threw down his scalpel and leapt onto the Afghan, knocking a surgical tech at Table Alpha to the floor. Mirabelle dropped her clipboard. "Captain Wallentine!" she screamed. "Sam! What are you doing?" The other surgeon backed up against the wall, still holding a needle in his suture forceps. The Afghan made a grab for the strap but because the man was so small it was easy for Sam to pin his hands above his head.

A heavy weight slammed into Sam's back. "Get control of yourself, sir!" said a burly Navy corpsman. He grabbed Sam's left wrist and pinned it behind his back.

Mirabelle grabbed his right hand.

"Sam, have you cracked?" she asked.

"Stop!" Sam protested. "Let go, and help me." They spun him around and dragged him to the door. An MP opened it for them. Sam felt like everything was moving in slow motion. His mind whirled as he fought to get the words out. "He's a suicide bomber! You just freed his hands and now he—"

The explosion wasn't a resounding boom like in the movies. It was an ear-splitting crack. A shock wave of heat and incredible light slammed into his back.

Sam awoke, lying prone on the gray, dusty soil. His head was tilted to the right. With one eye he could see American soldiers running in all directions. They paused, knelt and fired rifles above him. The firefight lasted only half a minute.

Someone put a hand on his shoulder. He tried to move, to roll onto his back, but he couldn't get his muscles to cooperate. Two fingers felt around on his neck. A voice called out, "This one's still alive. Medic, Medic, over here!" Sam's eyelid drooped and he slipped back into unconsciousness.

CHAPTER 1

$\mathcal{A}$ ndi sat at a table reading from her laptop to her best friend and boss Harper Boyce. "Let's see what the Clementine Connection has to say about our honored guest today."

"To hear folks tell it, you'd think a celebrity was coming to town rather than a new doctor." Harper's hand went to her hip as she wagged a finger. "I don't know why you bother reading that rag column. The gossip's only right half the time, no, not even half," Harper muttered as she busied herself around the dining room of The Magnolia Restaurant.

"Someone woke up on the wrong side of the bed this morning," Andi chided.

Harper straightened several sets of silverware then stepped back to examine her handiwork. "You'd be grumpy too if you'd gotten here at four a.m. this morning."

"You could've called me, and I would've come to help," Andi pouted.

Harper let out a long sigh. "I know you would have." Andi arrived a little after six. Harper hadn't asked the rest of the staff to get here until seven because she wanted to take care of some things herself. The tables had to be arranged just so. She set a long table at the front of the main dining room for the distinguished guest and the powers that be. The other tables she arranged to give all the guests a good view of the new doctor and he of them. Today was a big day in Clementine, Alabama, and The Magnolia had to positively shine.

Andi ignored Harper's prickliness and continued in the enamored tone of one who lapped up gossip like a kitten going for a bowl of milk. "According to Maryanne, 'As you all know we've been without a doctor for three years; ever since Vernon Stanley left town in the middle of the night under, shall we say, rather scandalous circumstances. Our dear Mayor Tate has been tirelessly searching for a replacement—'"

Harper grunted. "Tirelessly searching? That's slathering it on thick. The mayor spends most of his time on the golf course, that is, when he's not on vacation or relaxing in his Olympic-sized swimming pool."

"Hush! Let me finish reading. Where was I?" Andi paused to find her spot. "Oh, yeah." She cast Harper an annoyed look. "As I was reading, 'Our dear Mayor Tate has been tirelessly searching for a replacement. But in this day of urgent care clinics, hospitalists and huge physician networks, it isn't easy to find someone who'll come to our little town and be on call twenty-four hours a day, seven days a week.'"

Harper smiled a little at Andi's enunciation of the word *tirelessly*. She admired Andi's spunk, which was part of the reason they were close friends. *Birds of a feather flock together.*

"Sounds about like a restaurant owner," Harper interjected, but Andi ignored her and kept reading.

"'According to Mayor Tate, our new doctor is just leaving the Army. His name is Samuel Wallentine, MD. He's been treating battle casualties in Afghanistan for the past year, and that wasn't his first deployment, we understand. He's also gone on Army humanitarian missions to provide care to mountain tribes in Guatemala, remote islands in the Philippines, and isolated villages in Uganda.'"

Andi looked up from her laptop. "Wow, this guy gets around."

"A real angel of mercy," Harper said dryly.

"To hear Maryanne spout on, you'd think the good doctor was a candidate for sainthood," Andi giggled.

"See, more reason not to believe any of the drivel Maryanne writes."

Andi held up a finger. "Shh. I'm not finished. 'Mayor Tate says everyone is invited to the welcome ceremony at City Hall at ten. After that there will be a luncheon at The Magnolia.'" Andi's eyes rounded to saucers. "They better not expect lunch to be free though, right Harper?"

"That's right," Harper chirped, squaring her chin. She believed in giving back to the town as much as the next person, but she had bills to pay. She wasn't running a soup kitchen.

Andi got to the end of the post. "'Dr. Wallentine will be available to greet everyone during the luncheon. Best of all, he will start office hours at eight o'clock sharp on Monday morning. Who'll be first on the list to see him?'" Andi shook her head. "I wager Maryanne has already tried to get the first time slot, the old hypochondriac."

Harper laughed. "You said it, not me." The last tendrils of her grumpiness over lost sleep faded as her eyes surveyed the space. It looked great, if she did say so herself. Despite her nonchalant attitude about the doctor's arrival, Harper felt a tingle of excitement. She was proud that her establishment would be the center of today's hubbub.

While Harper's distaste for Maryanne Wheatley and her busybody blog soured her attitude about today's events, she understood why the doctor's arrival was big news.

Rarely did anyone move to Clementine, Alabama. Travelers on the Interstate sometimes stopped in for a bite or a gas fill-up on their way to the beach, but other than that, no new blood came in. Clementine was one of those delightful little towns where babies were born and grew up nurtured and protected by a closely knit community of friends and family. Sometimes, though, it was nice to pump some new energy into the ordinary.

Harper pushed her shoulder-length blonde hair off her forehead and straightened the tablecloth on the front table so that it was just right. The Magnolia was the town's showcase restaurant, famous for its sweet potato pie. The original owner of the restaurant Scarlett Breeland married a football star and moved to Atlanta, leaving The Magnolia in the highly capable hands of her cousin and trusted partner, Harper. She grinned inwardly knowing that if Scarlett heard her thoughts, she'd raise an eyebrow at her description of herself—*highly capable*. Harper did her best to hold things together. Of course, it helped that Harper loved this restaurant heart and soul. It was her baby.

The Magnolia had been a grand old family home for a local cotton broker, built a century earlier in the Roaring Twenties, before the Great Depression sucked prosperity out of the local and national economies. The restaurant's dining room had been the family's parlor. Scarlett had knocked down a couple of walls to enlarge the room but kept the original dark-stained knotty pine floors. Since the house pre-dated air conditioning and was older than the arrival of electricity in Clementine, the entire first floor was surrounded by windows.

Andi closed her laptop and stood. "Everything looks perfect, as usual."

"Thanks," Harper said offhandedly, "but it's not perfect yet. There are still a few things to do. I'll get the staff to take care of them when they arrive."

Andi stifled a yawn. "I'd better grab a bite to eat before things get crazy. You want me to make you something?"

"Nah, not right now." Harper was too keyed up to eat. She'd grab a piece of fruit or handful of nuts later.

"All right, but don't say I didn't ask," Andi sang as she reached for her laptop and traipsed to the kitchen.

Harper's thoughts went to the luncheon. She planned to position herself at a vantage point so she could see the entire audience and direct her servers to make sure everyone was impeccably attended to. Harper tried her best to run a tight ship. Every now and then a supplier or new employee tried to pull something over on the petite, blue-eyed blonde, and she had to put them in their place faster than a chicken on a night crawler. When she was done, they knew where

4

they stood, which was never taller than her five-foot-four-inch stature.

Seven o'clock came, and the rest of the employees arrived. "Morning, Harper," they chimed as they walked in.

"Hey. Everyone ready for the big day?" Harper didn't wait for an answer. "Peggy, a lot of the silverware came out of the dishwasher with spots. Why don't you start polishing it? Rodney, help her with that and wrap them as she gets them done. Andi, call Cindy Stubblefield and find out how the flowers are coming along. Marie, the overnight cleaning crew didn't do a good enough job in the front entry. Get the entryway mop and bucket and give it a proper going-over. Stanley, Frank, get started in the kitchen. You know what to do."

Everyone took their assignments and hustled off to work.

The Magnolia consumed most of Harper's waking time. In fact, it had cost her a couple of potential relationships. Those men had felt like they played second fiddle to her job. Before her most recent breakup with Warner Stein, she dated Hoyt Blankenship who had the audacity to make a snarky comment dissing her sweet potato pie, saying it was a puddle of mush. "Oh, you didn't just say that," she'd retorted. It was as if he'd said her baby was ugly. She immediately and forcefully educated him on the virtues of the pie. The grand finale of that tutorial being a pie in Hoyt's face; after which, he spent the next hour picking it out of his nose and mustache.

When the first set of chores was complete, Harper assigned new ones. "Marie, Rodney, polish all the goblets and glasses. Peggy, make sure the ice bins are all full. Andi, are the flowers here yet? Get them arranged on the tables. I want a big display on the mayor and doctor's table."

Eleven-thirty arrived. Right on schedule, Mayor Tate and the crowd climbed the front steps onto the wide Southern-style porch. They'd finished the welcome ceremony at City Hall and were here to be fed. The mayor's assistant held the door for him and the guest of honor. "Come on in, Dr. Wallentine. Oh, sorry. Come on in, Sam. This is the place I've been telling you about," the mayor said like he and the doctor were old friends.

Harper turned around to see the new arrival. She wasn't sure what she'd expected, but certainly not this man. A jolt ran through her. The doctor was easy on the eyes. A couple inches over six feet tall, he had chestnut-brown hair, an olive complexion, and enough muscle on him that it couldn't be overlooked. He looked uncomfortable with all the attention.

"Come on Sam, over here," Mayor Tate said as he waved to the opposite end of the dining room.

"Wow, he's a hottie," Andi said.

Harper elbowed her to shush, but Andi elbowed right back. A second later, Harper ducked into the kitchen doorway next to the server stand. She'd strategically placed a mirror just inside the kitchen so her girls could check their looks before delivering food to diners. It didn't do to have a sweaty wait staff. She wished she'd taken more time to get ready this morning. Then again, it had been three-thirty a.m. when she left her house. She fluffed her hair and smoothed her foundation. There were faint circles around her eyes. She winced. Nothing could be done about those right now. She grabbed a Pink Frosting lip gloss from her pocket and applied a fresh layer. One more check of the hair; she smoothed down a wild bundle winging up on her right side.

As soon as Harper walked back into the dining room, Mayor Tate called her over. "Harper, come meet our new doctor."

Harper's pulse bumped up several notches. The idea was to appear dignified. Harper thought of the rumors that had been flying for weeks about their new doctor. Andi pegged him as a middle-aged, portly, balding man with thick glasses and pale skin. Boy, had she missed the mark.

Dr. Wallentine had a masculine square jaw and thoughtful green eyes. He wore his polo shirt very well, the outline of his pecs clearly evident beneath it. The sleeves stretched pleasantly around his biceps. His brown hair was lush and wavy. His smile looked sincere if not a little bashful. It was kind of endearing.

Harper dodged a few customers to get around the crowd filing in for the welcome luncheon. The mayor's attention was pulled away by his assistant, leaving Harper to do her own introduction. She extended her hand. "Hi, Dr. Wallentine. I'm Harper Boyce. Welcome to The Magnolia."

He stood and knocked his chair over backward. Color rose in his cheeks as he reached to set it back upright.

Harper bit back a smile. It was nice to know that she wasn't the only one who didn't have everything completely put together. "Careful, that chair'll get you every time," she teased.

His eyes lit with a faint amusement as he grimaced. "My first casualty."

Harper laughed.

He cleared his throat. "Please, call me Sam." He was a full head taller than her. She looked up into his eyes, and he smiled nervously. His shoulders were so broad it seemed like he blocked the light coming in the window behind him. His hand swallowed Harper's petite one as he shook it. When their skin touched, a surge shot up Harper's arm. Sam's touch was warm with enough callus but not too much. A surgeon might have soft hands but his were obviously used to hard work.

Was it her imagination or had he held her hand a little longer than necessary? He was smiling at her, not a grin or a lecherous smile, but one that seemed to whisper, *I'd like to get to know you better.* A warm flush washed through Harper's chest. She tried to keep from blushing, but couldn't stop it. She smiled back, but when she tried to speak, her mind was blank and nothing would come out. Finally, she managed to say, "You too." You too what? That was a stupid thing to say. She bit her bottom lip and looked out the window for a second. Looking back, she smiled at him again.

"Is this your restaurant?" Sam asked politely.

"Yes, it is."

"I appreciate you going to all this trouble for me."

Harper waved a hand. "I was glad to do it." She was grateful that Sam had the good grace to appreciate her effort.

The mayor reinserted himself into the conversation with a glib, "Look at you, so appreciative of every little thing." He raised his voice so everyone around could hear. "Folks, our doctor here's a real gentleman, and he's not even from the South."

Harper bristled. Every little thing? Orchestrating a large luncheon was not a little thing! As her sleep-deprived mind tried to come up with something witty that would put the mayor in his place, Sam spoke.

"I didn't realize the South held the monopoly on manners." He arched his brow as he turned to the mayor.

Harper had to stifle the surprised chortle rising in her throat, especially when Mayor Tate's face went redder than an over-ripe tomato. She was liking Sam more and more.

The mayor cleared his throat as he squirmed like a hooked worm. "Uh, of course not. I didn't mean to imply …"

"No worries," Sam said pleasantly, sitting back down. He caught Harper's eye and gave her a subtle wink.

A smile tugged at Harper's lips, and for a split second, she felt like they were the only two in the room.

Unlike Sam, Mayor Tate failed to stand for Harper but thrust out his hand for a quick shake. An awkward moment passed. Harper couldn't think of anything halfway intelligent to say, so she turned away and pretended to survey her quickly filling restaurant. "Well, better get things moving." She waved to the wait staff. "Start taking orders, ladies."

Several minutes later, Harper walked into the kitchen and passed Marie, who was carrying a tray of waters.

Marie paused in her tracks. "Careful, or you'll chew that bottom lip off," she quipped.

Harper realized she was biting her lower lip again.

Marie studied her with astute eyes. "Not quite what you expected?"

Harper blinked. "What do you mean?"

Marie laughed. "You know exactly what I mean. It's written all over your face."

Heat flashed across Harper's cheeks and she had to fight the urge to fan herself. Was it obvious to the entire restaurant that she found the doctor attractive?

Marie lowered her voice. "It's okay, sugar. I won't tell a soul. I just happened to see you earlier when you were talking to the doctor. I have a sixth sense about these things," Marie said with a touch of pride. "If you need advice in the romance department, you can always talk to me."

Harper suppressed a laugh. Marie was middle-aged and on her third marriage, not the best candidate for handing out relationship advice. Still, Marie had a kind heart, and Harper didn't want to be catty. "Thanks, I'll keep that in mind," she said with a straight face.

"So, he's different than you thought?" Marie's eyes shone with interest.

Harper took a deep breath and let it out quickly. "I don't know that I had any expectations, per se."

Marie laughed. "I thought we'd be getting Mayor Tate's twin brother. Instead, he's ..." She shook her head. "Well, let's just put it this way ... if my Jimbo wasn't such a sweetie, I'd be trading him in for that hunk of a man," she purred. "Know what I mean?"

Frank the head cook pointed a carving knife at them. "Put a cork in it, Marie. Give the poor man time to get his feet on the ground before you start ogling him to death."

"I don't ogle," Marie countered with an indignant sniff.

Harper shook her head and smiled. Marie was something else. Realizing that they were wasting precious time, Harper clapped her hands. "All right, peeps. Enough dawdling. We've got a meal to serve."

The servers moved through the tables greeting local dignitaries and the just plain curious folks who'd come to check out the new doc. Andi was busy at the hostess stand, directing customers to open seats. When the steady flow of people trickled off, Harper stepped up beside Andi.

A wicked grin ruffled Andi's lips. "So, it seems I'm not the only one taken with the new doc."

Harper fast blinked. "Huh?"

Andi lowered her voice. "What was that all about?"

Harper frowned. "What was what all about?"

"I thought you were gonna faint when he shook your hand."

Harper felt her face turning red again. "Did not." *Sheesh.* At this point, she was the one turning into an over-ripe tomato.

"Did so."

"Did not, not, not," Harper sassed, her hands going to her hips. They giggled like a couple of middle school girls who'd just spotted a hunk on the beach.

Andi peeked around Harper to get another look at the guest of honor. "He's a fine specimen, isn't he? Oh, look at that!" Harper turned around as Andi continued. "He reached for his water with his left hand. He's left handed! You know what they say about left-handed men."

Harper made a face. "No, I don't. What do they say?"

Andi's eyes danced, her voice going juicy. "I don't know either but I'm sure it's good."

Harper grunted. "Come off it, Andi. You're already in a relationship."

"Yeah, but you're not."

"I imagine that he is. What guy who's been around long enough to finish college, medical school, surgery residency, and Army service is still going to be single?"

"Well, if his finger tells the truth, I'd say him. No ring and no tan line."

"Seriously? You managed to observe all that amid herding all these people to their seats?"

Andi laughed. "I've got skills."

"Evidently," Harper said tartly.

Harper stole a peek as Sam set down his water glass. Blotches crawled up her neck when he glanced up and caught her looking. Harper spun back around to face Andi. "He's a surgeon. They're not allowed to wear rings. It spreads germs in the operating room."

"Mmm hmm. You just keep telling yourself that, baby."

The servers had taken orders and were speedwalking across the room to get theirs into the kitchen ahead of everybody else's. "I'd better go help direct kitchen traffic for Frank and Stan. You behave." She gave Andi a wink and crossed the dining room to the kitchen door, stopping a few times along the way to acknowledge greetings from her regular customers.

The luncheon came off perfectly. An hour and a half later, customers began filtering out of the restaurant and back to their jobs. When Harper emerged from the kitchen, she felt like she'd come through the war and lived to tell the tale. Running a quick hand over her hair to smooth it, Harper approached the head table. Sam stood up again.

"That was excellent, ma'am. Thank you."

"If I'm to call you Sam, then don't be ma'aming me. It's Harper."

He smiled. His teeth were blinding and perfect. "Absolutely, Harper. I hope you'll let me come back and enjoy your cuisine again."

Mayor Tate interrupted. "You'll be welcome here anytime, doc. In fact, as you can see, your office is just half a block down on the other side of the street." He pointed out one of the big windows. "See? You can eat here every day."

"I particularly enjoyed the sweet potato pie, ma'am." There he went again with the *ma'am* thing. It must have been something the Army drilled into him. It was polite, but it made Harper feel like a grandma.

"It's the best around," Mayor Tate said before Harper could respond. "And trust me, I know my pie." He patted his ample midsection and got up from his chair.

Harper just smiled. The mayor pushed Sam by the elbow to navigate him toward the foyer. They walked a few steps in that direction before the mayor pointed to a woman in a bright flowered dress with a plunging neckline. The woman twisted her foot back and forth in her pink high heels as she smiled brightly at the man she was talking to. "She's the realtor I told you about. Pepper, come on over here," the mayor said with a wave.

The hair on the back of Harper's neck stood. Pepper McClain the nemesis of every wife in Clementine immediately lost interest in the man she'd been flirting with. She sashayed over to the mayor and Sam, not giving Harper even the slightest glance. Only twenty-five years old, Pepper already had two children, the older one now in the fourth grade. She'd been married to the younger child's father. No one other than Pepper knew who the older one's father was. After the two babies, she married a second time but that marriage was brief. She was openly canvassing for husband number three.

Andi stepped up beside Harper and put a calming hand on her shoulder. "Hold your horses there, girl. That bimbo's no match for you. If you're interested in this guy, Pepper can walk him through every house for sale in the county, and it won't do her a lick of good."

"Obviously, Warner didn't feel the same way." The words left a sour taste in Harper's mouth.

"Warner was a moron. You know Pepper can't compete with this." She pinched Harper's butt for emphasis, making Harper jump.

"Stop it," she said with a shake of her head as she laughed.

Pepper looked their direction and gave Harper a 'too bad for you' smile. Harper scowled back. Pepper's tight, strawberry blonde curls bounced as she glided up to Sam. He smiled at Pepper, but it was more of a bland, sterile smile like he was just being friendly. *Good for you, Sam. Keep it professional.*

"Hello, Dr. Wallentine," Pepper cooed in a sultry voice loud enough to be heard by the entire restaurant. "I understand you're in the market." Her insinuating tone left no doubt that she meant *on* the market. Harper's fingers itched to rip every strand of Pepper's over-processed curls out of her head. Even as the thought flitted through her mind, Harper mentally chastised herself for being catty. She had no reason to feel jealous. Sam was a customer and by first impression a decent person, but that was it.

Pepper slipped an arm through Sam's. Still gazing up at him like he'd hung the moon and stars, she asked without looking around, "Mayor Tate, are you done with the good doctor?"

"Yep. We've about wrapped everything up." The mayor thrust his thumbs through his front belt loops as he rocked forward on the balls of his feet. "Why don't you take Sam up to Hudson Bay Golf Course, and show him some nice places there?"

"So, he's all mine now. Great." Pepper dragged out the word *great*

12

and Sam's expression was clearly uncomfortable. Harper decided then and there that she liked the good doctor. She had the unreasonable urge to rescue him from Pepper's wiles, and then had to remind herself that Sam Wallentine wasn't hers to rescue.

"If you'll excuse me, I need to go to the kitchen and start getting things tidied up," Harper snipped. If she watched this scene any longer, she'd be sick to her stomach.

Pepper cast a snide glance at Harper and mouthed the word 'Cinderella.'

It took Harper a second to process what Pepper had just done. Seriously? Harper saw red!

Pepper shot Harper a condescending look and stuck her chin in the air.

Harper's blood boiled at the insult. Had the mayor and Sam not been here, Harper would've put Pepper in her place in two-seconds flat, reminding her that things didn't work out so well for the evil stepsisters. It was a good thing Andi stood next to her, or Harper would've been tempted to go after Pepper even in the presence of Sam and Mayor Tate.

"We have a couple of other nice subdivisions too, but Hudson Bay is the top of the line," Mayor Tate explained as they walked toward the door.

"I'll drive if you like," Pepper said, her words dripping like syrup.

"Thanks. That would be great. I'd just get lost," Sam replied.

"Don't worry. I'd always come find you," Pepper purred as she squeezed Sam's arm and pulled him close against her body before they walked out.

Mayor Tate followed and waved as they went down the front steps. "You kids have a good time," he boomed with a congenial smile. He looked pleased as punch with himself over how things were going. For some reason, this irritated the heck out of Harper. Why was she so irritated? Sam needed a place to live. It only made sense that he'd have to work with a realtor. Sure, Harper had felt some connection between them, but how much of that was wishful thinking on her part? As far as Sam was concerned, Harper was just one of the many faces he'd met today. Harper needed to see this thing for what it was. Sam came to Clementine to do a job. It was as simple as that. It was a good thing that Clementine had a new doctor. Harper should be happy instead of fighting mad. The insight came to her in a flash. The source of her annoyance could be summed up in two words—Pepper McClain.

"I'd give anything to strangle that floozy," Andi muttered.

Harper laughed in surprise, her mood lifting. "Get in line, sister." Harper noted that Sam didn't open Pepper's car door for her and didn't smile much after he sat down. Pepper lowered the convertible's top, put on her sunglasses, and drove off.

CHAPTER 2

Two days later, Clementine Medical Care reopened its doors, now under new management. Sam was able to hire the previous receptionist Felicia Jones and nurse Jan Clemens back from the hospital in Daphne, where they'd both gone to work after the previous doctor fled, or as it was told, was run out of town. He liked both his staffers from the get-go. Felicia was forty-five years old. A petite woman who was on the portly side, Felicia had short brown hair and dark, almond eyes that shone with an intelligent light. Jan, closer to fifty-five, was tall and reed thin with silver streaked, sandy hair. They'd both been born, raised, married, and would probably die in Clementine. The great advantage of that was that they could fill him in on everyone who came in the door; who they were related to, whether they were homebodies or carousers, the health of their parents and cousins, and when necessary, their criminal records. He was particularly interested, of course, in the previous doc, Vernie whatever-his-name-was. He worried a little that Vernie's reputation might be linked to the practice and didn't want it to tarnish his own.

Even though he was brand new, his first day's schedule was packed. Sam glanced over it to see who he was expecting. He wasn't trained in family practice. It had been over ten years since he'd delivered a baby. Hopefully it would all come back. Cindy Stubblefield, whose florist shop adorned every town function from weddings to funerals, was bringing in one of her boys for his kindergarten shots. Douglas Foster wanted to get his lungs checked. He'd been having some trouble ever since his house burned down two years ago. Sadie Lynn Armstrong needed refills on her diabetes medicine. She was dragging her husband Willie in for a physical, because he hadn't had one in nearly three decades. And on and on it went. Felicia scheduled him just two patients an hour on that first day, and it was a good thing she did. There weren't any quick visits. Everybody wanted to sit and chat with the new doctor.

Sam wore his white coat for the first couple of appointments but quickly decided he hated it. He always sat on his coat tails, and then when he leaned forward to stand up, it would choke him. How did women manage to function in dresses? The walls in the office didn't insulate sound very well. He tried to keep his voice down when patients brought up intimate details, but they usually didn't do the same, and he could picture the whole waiting room giggling over Mrs. Sikes's boisterous and detailed description of her hemorrhoids.

He soon discovered that his surgical skills wouldn't be wasted in this little town. By the end of the day, he'd scheduled two colonoscopies, a cyst biopsy, and Mrs. Sikes's hemorrhoidectomy at the hospital over in Daphne. He arranged an ultrasound so they could decide if Sadie Lynn needed to have her gall bladder taken out and a cystoscopy for Willie. This was going to be a good practice for him if it kept up like the first day, and maybe he would be good for these humble, likable people. They were rapidly growing on him.

Finally, as the sun was hovering over the horizon to the west, trying to decide whether to keep playing peek-a-boo behind the pink and golden clouds or dip out of sight, Sam emerged from his office and locked the door behind him. He glanced up and down the street. Not only was The Magnolia the best eatery in town. It was also the only eatery. Unless, that was, one could consider the Dixie Freeze a place for supper. He'd left his car at the Clementine Bed and Breakfast that morning, so he walked over to The Magnolia.

The bell on top of the etched glass door jingled merrily when he opened it and walked in. He hadn't paid much attention to the entryway at the luncheon. The rich brown floors and wall timbers gave a feeling of warmth and sturdiness. The plaster on the walls between the timbers was cream-colored and cozy.

Sam heard the voices before he saw to whom they belonged. The couple were so caught up in their conversation that they hadn't noticed Sam enter the restaurant. Instantly, he recognized the beautiful blonde, Harper. His thoughts had returned to her several times. He liked her sauciness when she teased him about knocking over the chair. An unexpected pang shot through Sam. Harper was obviously involved with someone, and the two were having what looked to be a lover's quarrel.

"I've already told you, Warner, the kitchen is closed." She glared at the man facing her.

Sam took a quick assessment of the man—thin, a little over six feet tall with a corporate haircut. The man was dressed in casual business attire that included khaki pants and a polo shirt. Maybe it was bad for Sam to make a first-glance judgment, especially since Sam was disappointed that Harper was taken, but the guy looked like an overgrown frat boy who thought life owed him a free pass. Sam's senses went on full alert when the man grabbed Harper's arm.

"This has nothing to do with the kitchen," the man argued. "It's about you and me."

"There is no 'you and me'. You need to leave!" Harper jerked her arm in an attempt to remove it from his grasp, but he held on tight. "Take your hand off me," she demanded.

The man grunted. "Or what?"

Sam stepped forward, intent on making his presence known. "Is there a problem here?"

They turned to him in surprise. A sneer twisted over the man's face. "This is none of your business."

"I'll decide what's my business." Sam tightened his fists as he looked at the man's hand around Harper's arm. One thing he couldn't tolerate was men using their strength to bully women.

"Who are you?" There was an insolent tone in the man's voice.

Sam's mind catalogued several things at once. One, he saw Harper's relieved expression and knew she was grateful he was there to help. Two, he was inches taller than the man and felt sure he could take him in a fight if he had to. Sam didn't go looking for a fight, but he'd learned a long time ago that the only way to face a bully was head-on. He looked the man in the eye, letting him know that he meant business. Uncertainty crept into the man's eyes as he released Harper's arm.

"I don't want any trouble," the man said.

"Good," Harper fired back, "then don't ever come here again."

"I love you." There was a hint of desperation in the man's voice as he searched Harper's face.

She drew herself up to her full height, a look of resignation coming over her features. "Goodbye, Warner, you know your way out."

Shaking his head in disgust, Warner stormed out of the restaurant.

"Thank you," Harper said with a wan smile.

"You're welcome." Sam looked at the red marks on her skin. "Are you okay?"

She looked down, rubbing her arm. "I'll live," she said dryly.

Sam glanced around at the chairs that were put up on the tables as he mentally replayed the conversation Harper just had with Warner. "I'm sorry, I didn't realize you were closed."

"Yeah, we shut down at eight or when the last supper customer leaves, whichever comes first."

He nodded.

"I understand. Next time I'll plan better."

A tall, slim brunette walked out of the kitchen. When she saw Sam, her face lit with recognition. "Dr. Wallentine. Hello." She held out her hand. "I'm Andi."

"Nice to meet you, Andi," he said as they shook hands.

"Are you here for dinner?"

Sam glanced at Harper. "Yeah, I was, but I didn't realize you guys were closed. I'll try again next time."

18

"Nonsense. Frank and Stan," Andi called loudly, "we've got one more customer."

"Oh no, I couldn't," Sam protested. "You all have kids to get home to."

An amused look passed between Andi and Harper. "So, we have kids now?" Andi drawled.

Harper chuckled, the tension lines in her face dissolving. "That's news to me."

Sam laughed, realizing they were teasing him.

Andi brought her hands together. "We need to get you something to eat."

"Yes, we do," Harper agreed, "it would be bad business to turn away the new doc hungry."

"I won't hold it against you … much," Sam added with a grin.

"I see how you operate," Harper said, her eyes smiling. She turned to Andi. "I've got this one. You go on home."

Sam didn't miss the subtle wink Andi gave Harper. Did that mean that Harper might have some interest? Sam realized with a jolt that he hoped so. He wondered about Harper's involvement with the man that had just left. Obviously, there was no love lost on Harper's part, but the guy was still hung up on her. Sam figured a woman like Harper had broken more than her fair share of hearts.

Andi went to the kitchen doors, pushed them open, and yelled. "Never mind about the customer. Time to clock out."

A busboy stuck his head out. "Clock out?" he asked wide-eyed. "Are we supposed to clock in and out?"

"It's just an expression," Andi said with an exasperated sigh. "It means we're leaving. Now move it." One by one, the wait staff shuffled out the door. Andi called into the kitchen, "Frank and Stan, you boys about done?"

"On our way," came the reply.

Harper turned to Sam. "You worked awfully late today. Vernon used to cut his schedule off by about two in the afternoon, so he could do his charting and other paperwork. He also figured he'd be taking care of people during the night every now and then, so he deserved shorter days."

Sam was surprised that Harper knew the ins and outs of Vernon's schedule. Then again, it was a tight-knit town. Everybody seemed to know each other like family. So far, Sam felt welcome. Felicia, Jan, Harper, Mayor Tate, even Pepper, seemed to be eager to make him feel at home. It was so different from New Jersey. Each time he came home on furlough for a visit, people made him feel like a stranger. Clementine felt more like coming home and finding the whole family on the couch watching a movie, and all of them moving over to make room for him.

Harper brought her hands together. "All right. Let's get you fed."

Sam felt like a charity case. "I really can go someplace else."

"Not a chance. Making you dinner's the least I can do, especially after that heroic display earlier."

"What heroic display?" Andi walked toward them, reentering the conversation so quickly that Sam realized she'd been listening to everything they were saying.

Harper waved a hand. "It's nothing," she said nonchalantly, giving Sam an appreciative smile. "Sam was kind enough to help me take out the garbage."

Sam liked that Harper called him by his first name.

Andi was confused. "What garbage?"

Two cooks emerged from the kitchen, slop-covered aprons and all. "Night, Harper. If you use anything, don't bother washing it up. We'll take care of it in the morning." Within seconds they were out the door.

"Goodnight," Andi chirped as she followed behind them. Before going through the door, she threw a sly glance at Harper. "Don't do anything I wouldn't do."

"I don't need that much latitude," Harper responded in a singsong voice that rose a chuckle in Sam's throat.

Andi made a face as she left.

What a close-knit crew. They worked for Harper, but they acted more like family. In fact, the whole town seemed that way. It felt strange to know that people were watching, and no doubt judging, everything Sam did. Yet at the same time, it was warm and welcoming. He was certainly an outsider here, but the town seemed to be opening its arms wide for him. He could get used to this, as long as they didn't try to get too far into his personal business.

Harper went and locked the door before turning back to him.

"Well, sir, what'll it be?"

"I haven't been called *sir* since I left Walter Reed," Sam said. "Mind if I take a look at the menu?"

She chuckled. "The night menu might be a little scant, but let's see what we can scrounge up."

"I don't want to be any trouble," he repeated.

A wicked grin flitted at her lips. "You keep saying that. Are you trouble, Sam?"

He chuckled, noticing how the light dancing in her eyes turned them to glittering sapphires. "Only when it comes to protecting fair maidens from scandalous villains."

Her eyes widened as she laughed. "My knight in shining armor. Thanks for coming to my rescue earlier."

"Was that guy an old boyfriend?"

Shadows passed over her features. "Yeah. We broke up months ago, but Warner can't seem to get the message."

The fierce protectiveness which swelled in Sam's chest took him by surprise. "If you need my help with the delivery, you just say the word." To have just met Harper, he was certainly taking a keen interest in her.

Harper gave him an appraising look. "I'll have to keep that in mind." A smile tugged at her lips. "You're pretty tough for a doctor. I'll have to keep my eye on you."

" I hope so," he uttered.

Surprise washed over her features, making him fear that he'd misread her signals and overstepped. Then, she rewarded him with a dazzling smile that sent a surge of electricity through him. He really liked this woman.

She waved an arm. "Come on into the kitchen." He followed her, his eyes tracing the outline of her delicate shoulders and slim waist. He liked the gentle curve of her hips and how her glossy hair bounced with her every step. She pointed to her right. "There's a shelf full of tortilla chips. We can do up some nachos if you like those. I've got a few cans of soup in case of an emergency, but we don't actually serve them. I make the soup from scratch." She pulled open the walk-in cooler door. "Got some nice roast beef left from dinner. There's some leftover linguine we can toss up with shrimp. Those pork chops were really good. Let's see, what else?"

Sam followed her into the walk-in. It wasn't just Harper's beauty that intrigued Sam, but also her confidence and poise. It had been over a year since he'd been in a relationship, so he wanted to be cautious and not let loneliness dictate his actions. The last time he'd gotten serious with someone she seemed sincere, but as soon as he'd left for his pre-deployment training, Miranda Dear Johned him in favor of a Navy man. Navy! That was just unforgivable.

Sam picked up a couple slices of American cheese and a block of butter. "How about a grilled cheese sandwich?"

"Seriously? You're here with a chef, and that's all you want?"

A grin slid over his lips. "Gourmet grilled cheese. Yum." He set the ingredients on the prep board. She got a knife and shaved off thin layers of butter that she pressed onto the bread.

She sighed. "All right. Grilled cheese it is." She looked at the ceiling utensil rack. "Grab me that cast-iron skillet, would you?"

"Sure." Sam reached for the skillet and set it down on the stove with a soft clank. He watched as Harper turned the gas on high and placed the bread on the cast iron. The corners of her mouth turned up in an impish grin. It piqued his curiosity. "What are you smiling at?"

"You know, you could afford anything you want to eat, and I could probably make just about anything for you. I think it's funny that all you want is grilled cheese."

"I like to keep things simple." He figured Harper would appreciate that. She seemed elegantly simple. She spoke her mind. He liked that. She was independent and self-confident with a natural, unvarnished beauty much more attractive than the Barbie Doll women who lived in a plastic surgeon's office. Her neatly trimmed nails were short and unpainted, the way they should be for someone who prepares food for customers. Even after a hard day's work, Harper looked terrific. She carried on a good conversation but wasn't overbearing. Harper probably had a long list of guys vying for her attention. He wondered about Warner. What had gone wrong between them?

A few minutes later, two sandwiches were sizzling. Harper flipped them over in deft movements when they were just right and slid them onto a plate. "Ready?"

"Yeah. Thanks. You really didn't have to do this." Before she could complain about him beating a dead horse, he added, "But I'm glad you did." A smile broke over his lips.

Harper just shook her head and laughed.

He ripped one sandwich in half and took a bite. "Come on out here," Harper said walking into the dining room. "What would you like to drink?"

"How about Dr. Pepper?"

Harper went over to the soda fountain and got him a drink while Sam removed two chairs from a table. They sat down across from each other.

"So, how did Mayor Tate find you?" Harper began.

"I was in Walter Reed recovering. They have this newsletter that goes out, and one day there was an announcement about this little town looking for a new doctor to take over an existing practice. I was about to be busted loose from the hospital and the Army. I wanted a nice, quiet place to keep recuperating. I'm cooling it here and twice a week I head over to Fairhope for physical therapy."

She tilted her head. "Recuperating from what?"

He took a deep breath then another bite. Harper didn't say anything, and he got the feeling she was giving him the space he needed to get the words out.

"I was part of an advance hospital unit, which consisted of four shipping containers, each staging four operating tables and fully equipped to function independently. They don't always put four of them in one base, but there was so much fighting in the neighborhood that the higher ups thought it was a good idea. We received casualties straight off the battlefield, stopped the bleeding and sent them to big hospitals that patched them up more permanently, and then sent them to other hospitals in Germany or the US."

"So, were you ever sent into combat?"

He shook his head, the terror of the experience cloaking him. His throat grew dry as he swallowed, and then took a sip of his drink. "It came to us." Sam didn't like talking about what had happened, because it brought everything back, bringing up the painful question—Could he have stopped the explosion? Had he gotten his words out sooner, perhaps ... He sucked in a breath, willing his muscles to relax. Berating himself over what happened wasn't going to change anything. Sam's intellect knew that he wasn't to blame for the suicide bombing. His heart ... Well, that would take time to work through, but it wasn't going to happen tonight.

Sam looked across the table and realized that Harper was studying him. When their eyes met, she gave him a slight smile. Her expression was a combination of interest and compassion. Also, Sam felt her patience as she waited for him to put his thoughts into words. Sam sensed that Harper was the type of person that he could confide in, even though they'd just met.

He forced his voice to sound calm, as if he were relating something that he'd read about in a newsfeed—something that happened to some other poor, unfortunate soul. "A suicide bomber came in pretending to be wounded. They stuck him on the table next to mine. When he pulled the trigger, he blew the roof right off our operating room. Half of my unit was killed in the attack. I only survived because I was standing in the doorway. The explosion blew me out of the metal box we were operating in and clear of the flames." He thought of Sergeant Mirabelle, how the two of them had been exchanging witty banter about the pink gloves. There was Alisha, the medic with a husband and three children. Sam could only imagine the devastation Alisha's family experienced when they heard the news. "I imagine that if I'd been anywhere else, I'd have been killed with the rest of them. Our hospital had those three other ORs-in-a-can. They took what was left of me straight to surgery in the one right next door and put the pieces back together. When I was stabilized, they shipped me up the chain to Bagram, then to Germany. For the past four and a half months, I've been at Walter Reed learning to walk again." He exhaled, relieved to have gotten the words out. He realized that he was clenching his jaw. So much for his attempt to keep his narrative dispassionate.

"Holy cow. That's terrible."

Sam realized he was staring at his sandwich, when the touch of her hand on his shook him back to the present. He looked at her, the futile anger burning through him like acid. "No. What's terrible is the other eight people who didn't make it." He thought of his friends and coworkers—their hopes and dreams, snuffed out in an instant. "The coward killed the OR team that was working on him, our charge nurse, and the other three soldiers on my team. There were two more teams at the opposite end of the trailer. They came out alive but were burned, had their eardrums ruptured, lost eyes… I think I came out pretty good compared to them."

Harper's face paled with shock, making Sam regret speaking so frankly about the explosion and the devastation it wreaked. "Do you think about them a lot?" Harper asked in a small voice.

"Yeah, sometimes. I spent a lot of time with the shrinks in Germany and at Walter Reed. They're used to this kind of stuff. They said I should have huge mental wounds, big time PTSD and stuff, but they said I really don't." He offered a humorless smile. "Sometimes, I feel like the shrinks are right." He spread his hands. "Other times …" He shrugged. "All I know is that it still cuts."

She nodded in understanding. "I'm sorry," she said quietly.

He shrugged. "I guess we all have burdens to carry."

"It's called life."

Her frank response caused his spirits to lift. "I guess that's why they say life is a four-letter word."

She laughed in surprise. "I guess so." They shared a smile.

He looked down at his food. "You thought you were just making me a bite to eat. You didn't realize you were gonna get the nitty gritty of my full life history."

"I don't mind," she said frankly, and he could tell from her sincere expression that she didn't. It was nice to feel such a strong connection with someone. Sam hadn't felt that in a very long time.

"Are you going back?" she asked.

"No. I want to, but the Army insists their surgeons have all their fingers and toes." He held up his right hand, smiling wryly as he wiggled what was left of his pinky finger. "They wouldn't let me in the reserves or anything." Frustration pinged through him. He'd spent seven years giving his everything in the service of his country and in the blink of an eye, it was over. His talents were no longer wanted, all because he was missing part of his pinky finger.

"The loss of a pinky finger doesn't define a man," Harper said, her eyes meeting his with an open admiration that was refreshing and a bit unsettling. Was Sam ready for a relationship? Before coming to Clementine, he would've answered a resounding no to that question. But here, with Harper, he was having to rethink his stance.

Sam finished eating and leaned back in his chair. He realized that he'd spent the last little while droning on about himself and the sordid explosion. Harper probably thought he was a real downer. She, on the other hand, was intriguing. Back in Jersey when people heard a Southern accent they assumed the speaker was an uneducated hick. Harper proved them wrong. She was a lot more than a beautiful face. She was articulate, skilled, compassionate, inquisitive, and, he hated to admit it, but so far, she seemed perfect. He had to find out more. "What about you?"

She tipped her head causing the ends of her blonde hair to fall softly over her shoulders. "What about me?"

He liked the intelligent light in Harper's lively azure eyes. Sam couldn't remember the last time he'd enjoyed talking to anyone this much. "Well, I know your name. I know you own this restaurant. I know you don't have a problem showing weasels to the door."

"If the situation warrants," she inserted, eyes narrowing.

"I know you wouldn't let a man go home hungry." He sat back in his seat, spreading his hands. "That's about it."

She took in a deep breath "Let's see … where to begin?"

"How about with Warner?" he prompted.

"Ah, Warner." She pursed her lips. "Okay, the short story is that Warner met someone else and dumped me."

"I'm sorry."

She flicked her hand. "It's fine. I got over it. Unfortunately, Warner has decided that he wants me back." Fire flashed in her eyes, turning them stormy blue. "It's not happening," she said, squaring her jaw.

"Remind me to never get on your bad side."

She laughed, her features relaxing. "Okay, onto the next topic. Actually, I'm not the sole owner of The Magnolia. My cousin Scarlett and I are partners in the business."

"So," he mused, giving her a playful grin. "Who's the genius behind that sinfully good sweet potato pie?"

Harper laughed. "I can't take credit for the recipe. That was all Scarlett." She held up a finger. "However, I can take credit for coining the phrase *Home of the Ten Thousand Dollar Sweet Potato Pie*."

"I saw that over the front door and wondered about it."

"Do you follow NFL football?"

"A little."

"Are you familiar with Rocket Breeland?"

"He's the starting quarterback for The Georgia Patriots."

"That's Scarlett's husband."

"Mayor Tate mentioned Rocket Breeland a few times when expounding on the perks of Clementine." It was more than a few times, but Sam didn't want to throw the mayor under the bus by pointing it out.

Harper's eyes sparkled in amusement. "Yep, that sounds about right. Mayor Tate loves to name drop." She shook her head. "I'm sure the mayor did mention Rocket. From the way Mayor Tate carries on, you'd think that he and Rocket were joined at the hip." She waved a hand. "Anyway, the reason I brought up Rocket is because he once bid ten thousand dollars on Scarlett's pie at a charity auction."

"Wow. That's a lot of money for a pie."

A wistful smile curved her lips. "Rocket bought a lot more than a pie that night. That was the first step in his quest to win back Scarlett.

Of course, he did have a little help from my end, but that's another story for some other time."

Harper was spunky and down-to-earth. Sam liked that about her. It was cute to watch her brag about helping Rocket and Scarlett get together. "You and Scarlett seem close."

"We are." Her features tightened. "Scarlett and I have been through a lot together."

"What happened?" After asking the question, Sam remained silent. It was his turn to give Harper space to formulate her thoughts. He could tell from the way Harper's jaw worked that she was trying to decide how much she wanted to tell him. He realized in that moment that he wanted to learn everything he could about this fascinating woman.

"Our mothers are sisters." She hesitated. "Or at least they were." She shifted in her seat as if collecting her thoughts. Their eyes met across the table as Sam silently willed her to continue. "Almost twenty years ago, our parents were driving back from a meeting in Montgomery. Scarlett's dad got an award of some kind from the state CPA society. My aunt and uncle invited my parents to drive over with them for the award acceptance banquet and left Scarlett and me with a babysitter. On their way home, a drunk driver was going the wrong direction on the highway, and…" She looked down at her lap.

It was Sam's turn to put his hand over hers. He marveled at the warmth and softness of her skin, and how immensely he enjoyed the sparks between them. Perhaps the attraction was intensified by their mutual pain. "I'm sorry. When I hear stories like yours, I realize that I have no right to complain about what I've been through. Do you miss them a lot?"

Harper shrugged, keeping her gaze fixed on their hands. Was Harper uncomfortable with his touch, or did she, too, feel this strong connection? Her voice took on a faraway tone. "I was six years old. I remember them but not very well. Scarlett was eight. She had nightmares for years afterwards …" She paused, staring into the distance. Then, she blinked, offering an apologetic smile as her voice grew practical.

COOKING WITH THE DOC

Casually, she withdrew her hand from his, making him wonder if he'd overstepped the bounds. "By the time we got to be teenagers, Scarlett and I had moved on. Scarlett grew up with our Grandpa Douglas, and I moved in with my dad's sister's family." Her features softened. "They're amazing. I loved living with them. They're still in town, but my brothers and sisters ... well, their kids have either moved away or gone off to college." She flashed a smile that radiated the practical nature of one used to picking herself up and moving forward. "No need to feel sorry for me, doc," she said with a cavalier wink. "I'm not the one who got blown to smithereens."

Sam chuckled. "I knew there was a chance that would happen, and I signed up anyway. The Afghan War was already going on when I called my recruiter and asked the Army to pay for medical school. They were more than happy to do so. I expected to give them seven years, and then get out, but after being in for a little while, I decided to make a career of it. The suicide bomber spoiled those plans." He looked into her moist, sky-blue eyes. His questioning had brought out emotion, and he felt a pang of guilt for that. "You know, for the first time since I left the army, I'm thinking it might not be a bad thing to be here."

Harper blushed. "I'm sure lots of folks in Clementine are offering prayers of thanks that you're here."

"How about you?"

She blinked in surprise before a smile touched her lips. "I've certainly enjoyed the conversation."

"Me too."

He'd had relationships before. Short flings just for fun and some more serious. In his lonely moments, Sam still thought about Janice from his second and third years of college. He wouldn't have minded if that had turned permanent, but they grew apart, and she moved on without him. Then there was that redheaded lab tech at med school. He was smitten over her until he started seeing charges on his bank account he didn't recognize. That ended fast. But, Miranda who'd dumped him right before his deployment to Afghanistan had hurt him worst. Sam was still smarting over it. Maybe this wasn't a good time to be opening up to someone new. Or maybe it was. Harper had obviously been hurt before. She could appreciate the value of loyalty in a relationship.

He brushed the crumbs from his shirt and stood up to take his plate into the kitchen.

"Don't worry about that," Harper said. "Frank said he'll take care of it in the morning."

"I'll just wash it up fast in the sink. Won't take more than a minute."

"Don't bother. The health department won't let us wash in the sink. It all has to go through the sanitizer," Harper said.

Sam had no idea whether the regulations really said that, but he walked into the kitchen and set his plate and cup in the sink without washing them.

"Thanks again, Harper, for the food and the company," he said when he came back out of the kitchen.

She flashed a smile. "No, thank you. I enjoyed the company."

A warm sensation flowed through his chest when their eyes met.

"Ready?" he asked.

"Sure. Let me get my keys and lock up."

She retrieved her purse from the server station and pulled out her key.

On the front porch of the restaurant he hesitated awkwardly. Well, come to think of it, with anyone else it would have been awkward, but with Harper it wasn't. She had an ability to put him at ease. Being with her was warm and soft like snuggling into a fluffy down comforter kind of comfortable. Or sleeping in on Saturday morning while the sun beams in your window kind of comfortable. But it was thrilling, too, like Sam had been given a special pair of glasses that made the ordinary extraordinary.

Sam was surprised to learn that Harper lived a stone's throw from The Magnolia. They walked the three blocks to her house. He looked it over. It was a little white cottage with a welcoming front porch.

"Thanks for the escort home," Harper said. "I wasn't expecting that. Where's your car?"

"I left it at the bed and breakfast. I'll probably see you sometime tomorrow."

"Sounds good," she said. "I'll look forward to it."

His gaze traced the curve of her jaw, a longing to discover the taste of her lips welling inside him. "Yeah. Good night."

Creases formed around her eyes as she smiled, evidence of laughter and living. Sam was itching to discover the spice that flavored Harper with such a fascinating combination of feistiness and vulnerability. "Night."

Sam watched her close the door and turn off the porch light before turning to walk back to the bed and breakfast. He felt like he was walking a foot off the ground. The street lights cast a soft green glow on the ground that seemed like the most beautiful color he'd ever seen. The gardenias from the nearby bushes smelled better than anything he'd smelled before. Even the rhythmic squawking of katydids was the sweetest concert nature could have performed. The breeze coming up from the Gulf a few dozen miles away had never been more balmy.

Life was good, and it was all because of an extraordinary woman named Harper Boyce.

CHAPTER 3

*S*am wasn't accustomed to the way civilian hospitals operated. He'd spent the vast majority of his military career in small mobile hospitals, so the fourteen-bed hospital in Daphne worked just fine. It even had two ICU beds. The labor and delivery suite had one bed. When two moms came in to deliver, as happened from time to time, one of them had to labor in a regular hospital room.

The hospital staff knew how to be flexible. The drive back and forth between Clementine and Daphne wasn't too bad. On his first day, as Sam went to make his rounds, a deputy pulled him over for speeding through the dense pine forest highway from Clementine. Once the officer learned who he was, on subsequent days he still hit Sam's Lexus with his radar gun but just waved as he went past. Sam figured the deputy must not want to make an enemy of the only surgeon around. For his part, Sam wanted to be friends with the law, so he made sure not to go too far over the speed limit.

Sam was used to nurses, whom he outranked in the Army, standing out of respect when he entered the unit. These nurses merely looked up and smiled. It was just as well. It always made Sam uncomfortable when a woman offered him her chair. In that respect, the civilian world was actually better. Sam didn't need or expect respect merely because of his rank.

He spent the day in the OR and did his afternoon rounds. He was done by three o'clock. By four, he was back in his Clementine office. "What did I miss, Felicia?"

"Hiya, doc. Let's see." She pulled out her message book. "The drug reps have already heard you're here. They want to take you to lunch."

"For future reference, they can bring lunch in and feed the whole office, but I'm not going out to eat with some pretty young thing I don't even know." He thought of Harper and how she fit the bill of a *pretty young thing*, but he'd been more than happy to spend time with her. Still, that was different ... personal. Harper wasn't trying to sell him anything. "If the reps are willing to bring enough for all three of us, I'll listen to their pitches. For that matter, I'm no sexist. If I won't go out with a female rep, I can't go out with the guys either."

There was a hint of admiration in Felicia's expression as she nodded. "Good to know. Mrs. Allen wants to know if you'll prescribe ADD medicine for her boys. If I were you, I'd say no. Those kids are as normal as can be. My daughter teaches Jacob's fourth grade class, and his grades are just fine. He's just behaving like a boy."

Sam smiled. It sure came in handy having a receptionist who knew everybody. "Anyone else?"

"Nancy Sonneman is hoping you'll start prescribing her oxycodone, so she doesn't have to drive all the way to Fairhope for it. She takes four pills a day, six on some days."

"Kindly tell Nancy Sonneman that if she wants to discuss her pills, she'll need to come in for an examination. I'm not going to make doling out pills at random a part of my practice."

Another nod of admiration.

"That's about it."

Jan emerged from the back. "Hey there, doc. I just pulled all of yesterday's instruments out of the antiseptic soak, wrapped them, and put them in the sterilizer. I'm about ready to wrap it up. How about y'all ?" She ran a quick hand through her board-straight, shoulder-length hair before giving it a quick toss.

33

"We're done. Let's head out."

Felicia turned out the lights and, as she did so, glanced out the window with a grimace. "Uh oh. Mr. Foster's checking out your car."

Jan stepped up beside Felicia. "I wonder what that old goat's up to."

"Maybe he's just interested in cars," Sam piped in.

Felicia's head swung back and forth as she frowned. "No, it's more than that. Douglas hates everybody, except his neighbor Coralee Breeland."

"But he's sweet on Coralee, so that doesn't count," Jan added.

"True," Felicia said with a throaty chuckle. "If you look up the word *curmudgeon* in the dictionary, you'll find a picture of Douglas. If I were a betting woman, I'd say Douglas isn't happy about an outsider moving to our town. Be careful."

"That's right," Jan said, "you need to watch out for that one."

Sam grew thoughtful. "I remember Douglas from our first day in business. He's definitely not a warm and fuzzy kind of guy. Thanks for the warning."

"Anytime," Felicia chirped.

"Night, ladies."

"Night," they said in unison as they left the office. A few minutes after, Sam went out the front door and locked it. He held onto the railing as he descended the three concrete steps to the sidewalk. His knees were still tender and his gait slightly wobbly from the bombing, but the physical therapy was helping. Sam hoped that in time, he'd have a full recovery.

Mr. Foster eyed Sam as he approached before drawing himself up to his full tall, scrawny height. With his cane, he tapped the license plate on Sam's car. "Purple heart?"

"That's right," Sam answered with a touch of pride. "Afghanistan, 2019."

Foster snapped to attention, quite impressively for his years. He drew his right arm to a perfect salute. "Staff Sergeant Douglas Foster, 101st Airborne Division, Vietnam War, 1968. Took half a pound of shrapnel in my chest and belly at Hamburger Hill. A combat surgeon saved my life. I presume that was your job?"

Sam returned the salute. "Yes, it was, Sarge. Thank you for your service."

"And you for yours, sir." Douglas Foster lowered his arm. Without another word, he crossed the street and got into his old pickup. The engine turned over half a dozen times before it caught with a deep throaty hum.

Sam watched him go. How odd. Douglas Foster's reputation was being a cranky old nuisance, but here was something that was important to him. Sam mentally tucked that away for future use. He glanced down the street to The Magnolia, surprised and pleased to see Harper on the front porch. The past few times Sam had eaten at The Magnolia after work, he'd hoped to see Harper, but she hadn't been there. So, he'd tried to think up some plausible excuse to stop by her house. Now, here she was. A jolt of adrenaline shot through Sam as he increased his pace, trying to smooth out his steps to compensate for the slight limp.

"What was that all about?" Harper asked when he climbed the steps. "Was Grandpa Douglas giving you a hard time about something?"

"Not at all. He was pleasant, actually."

Harper looked up and down the street, her expression going dubious. "Must've been a trick of the light. I thought you were talking to Douglas Foster, but obviously not," she teased.

He laughed. "Douglas seems like a nice guy. You know, I kind of understand why he's so protective of this town and of you. Loyalty runs deep in him."

Harper gave him an appraising look. "Well said, doc. Grandpa Douglas has a good heart. Unfortunately, few people get to see it because his outsides are pricklier than a bucket of porcupines."

Sam grinned. Harper's open manner was like getting a whiff of clean, mountain air. He cleared his throat, shifting his weight from one foot to the other.

"I was operating today at the hospital in Daphne so I have the car. Want a ride home?"

Humor touched her features. "All three blocks?"

Heat rose into his face as he realized his blunder.

A teasing smile curved her lips giving her a girlish quality. "If you wanna spend time with me, Sam, just say so."

Surprised laughter rumbled in his throat. "You don't beat around the bush, do you?"

She perched a hand on her hip. "I figure it's better to be straight. Saves a lot of time that way."

It only took him half a second to articulate a response. "All right, I'd like to spend time with you." There. That was much easier than trying to come up with some piddly excuse for stopping by her house.

She rewarded him with an enchanting smile. "I thought you'd never ask. Let me get my purse, and I'll be back in a jiffy."

When she returned, they walked to his office. Sam opened her door and helped her into the passenger seat.

"You really are a gentleman," Harper murmured appreciatively. "Where to?" she asked when he sat down behind the wheel.

Sam felt like he'd scored some grand prize by having Harper beside him. Then, it dawned on him that he needed a place for them to go. "Want to see the houses Pepper's been showing me?"

The vibe immediately shifted to something cool as Harper frowned.

"We could do something else instead," Sam inserted, wondering why she'd suddenly gone frosty. Things had been going so well, but he'd obviously made a misstep somehow.

"No, I'd like to see the contenders."

"You sure?" He searched her face, thinking of how exquisite she was with her even features that boasted high cheekbones brushed with a touch of color. The crowning touch was her clear blue eyes that reminded him of a cloudless June sky. Sam still couldn't believe his good fortune in meeting Harper and learning that she was single. Was it possible that after all his travails, fortune was finally smiling down on him? Now, the trick was not to mess it up!

"Absolutely." She offered him a wide smile, and the warmth was restored so instantaneously that Sam wondered if he'd only imagined the negative mood shift. Maybe he was looking too deep into things, being paranoid because of his past failed relationships. Sam wanted to find someone with whom he could connect—someone to build a life with. Was Harper that someone? His pulse quickened at the notion.

As they drove north out of town to Hudson Bay Country Club, Harper cast a surreptitious glance in Sam's direction, her gaze lingering on the plane of his strong jaw. She could tell that Sam had been confused about her vehement reaction to the mention of Pepper's name. What Sam didn't know was that Pepper had come into The Magnolia several times, bragging about the large amount of time she was spending with Sam.

The sunset made a splendid show of fiery orange and brilliant blue, washing everything in mellow gold as they drove into the upscale neighborhood comprised of nice, new, spacious homes surrounded by the greens. A clubhouse was under construction near the parking lot.

Sam pointed. "Over there's one that I've been looking at. The owner hasn't even been in it for a year. He wants out and fast."

It was an imitation of a plantation mansion with a large wrap-around porch and a soldier's row of sturdy columns.

"Kind of a lot for a single guy, don't you think?"

"Yeah, but Pepper said I can get a great deal on it because the guy's desperate to sell."

Pepper. Harper's blood simmered at the mention of that loathsome woman's name. It was common knowledge in Clementine that Pepper was hot to trot on the lookout for her next husband. At The Magnolia, Harper had heard many a tongue, especially the female variety, wagging with disdain over how scantily Pepper dressed and her overt pursuit of the opposite sex.

Initially, Harper didn't put much stock in the gossip, figuring that much of it was owed to jealousy on the part of the women. After all, Pepper was an attractive woman. However, Harper's distaste for Pepper grew exponentially when Pepper set her sights on Warner

Stein, an out-of-town business consultant who'd come to Clementine for a six-month stretch.

Warner and Harper had been dating at the time. Their relationship was starting to get serious with them contemplating marriage. Then, Pepper turned Warner's head. Soon after, Warner realized that he'd made a colossal mistake and wanted Harper back, but it was too late. The damage was done. From that time on, Harper had Pepper's number. The feeling was mutual with Pepper viewing Harper as competition. Pepper never missed an opportunity to flaunt her latest exploits in Harper's face. Harper had no doubt that Pepper was lying awake at night, dreaming up ways to ensnare Sam in her crafty web.

The last thing Harper wanted was to get involved with another man who stood a chance of falling for Pepper's wiles. Harper had been left on her rear-end too many times in the past to go through it again. The smart thing to do would be to cut bait and just move on, especially if Sam had a thing for Pepper.

Sam turned left onto a cul-de-sac with four houses under construction. "See that one straight ahead? Pepper says its design would make it a great bachelor pad. There's a trail from the backyard that goes to the pool by the clubhouse. It's going to have a huge back porch where a bunch of us can get together and watch people tee off at the seventh hole."

A thundercloud of irritation gathered over Harper as she folded her arms tightly over her chest. Sickening images of Pepper ran through Harper's mind: Pepper holding onto Sam's arm, walking through the house explaining the floor plan … and hoping one day it would be her home with him, her little minions running through it destroying the place. Harper realized with a start that Sam was looking at her funny, probably because she wore a plus-size scowl on her lips.

"Don't let Pepper talk you into anything you don't really want," she warned. "She's out to make a sale, and she'll try to get you to buy what she thinks you should have. Make sure it's the right one for you." There. It sounded like she was talking about houses.

"Of course I won't. You're right, Pepper can be kind of pushy. And

I think she's a bit flirty too."

"You think?" she grunted. Harper had to fight the urge to laugh.

A *bit* flirty? Good grief, guys could be so blind sometimes. This one was supposed to be smart. "You don't want to get into a relationship you're going to regret later. With a house, I mean." She bit her lower lip. That was a Freudian slip if there ever was one.

The dimming light caused the Lexus's automatic headlights and GPS screen to come on. "It's starting to get dark. You probably have an early morning. I'd better get you home."

"I'm good for a little longer if you want." Despite her internal warning about staying away from Sam, Harper wasn't ready for the evening to end. Before Sam had started droning on about Pepper, things had been going well. Harper had hoped that Sam would come back into The Magnolia so the two of them could talk. Andi said he had come in, but as rotten luck would have it, Harper had been off those evenings. Today, Harper's luck had improved. She happened to be out on the front porch of The Magnolia, having just gotten something out of her car, when she spotted Sam talking to Grandpa Douglas. Now, she was riding around with him and had his undivided attention, but she was so ticked about Pepper that she was ruining everything. Even as the thoughts ran through her mind, she had to laugh at herself. She was pathetic. What was this? Some parody scene out of the old movie, *Doc Hollywood*? Just because a new doctor moved to town didn't mean she had to fall head over heels. Hadn't she just told herself that she was taking a hiatus from dating?

"I don't have any more houses to show you. Pepper took me to a couple of others, but I turned them down. I really don't need five bedrooms."

Yeah, but Pepper and her kids would love that. Good grief! Harper had to quit thinking about Pepper.

Harper forced her voice to sound cheerful. "Thanks for showing me the prospects." She looked at his large, rugged hands on the steering wheel. Harper had always liked tough men, but with that toughness often came fool-headed ignorance. Harper had culled many a good-looking guy from the list because he couldn't carry on a conversation that extended beyond football, beer, and Nascar. Sam had the wonderful, rare mix of being both manly and intelligent. *Warner was intelligent too*, the little voice in her head argued, *and he turned out to be a sucker for a bubble-headed bimbo with the morals of an alley cat. And for what? A flash-in-the-pan good time with a tight skirt?* Harper pushed aside the intrusive thoughts. She'd been crazy about Warner, but when he dropped Harper for Pepper, all her faith in men had gone down the toilet. A dark cynicism had crowded out her optimism. Harper continued to date because of the social aspect, but she was starting to wonder if there were any good guys left in this old world.

"You bet," Sam answered casually.

Silence drifted between them, and Harper wondered if she'd completely blown her chance with Sam. The two of them had really connected that night she made him the grilled cheese sandwiches. Harper was touched that Sam had shared those personal things about his past, which prompted Harper to share her experiences.

"Do you ever manage to break away from the restaurant?"

"Every once in a blue moon," she quipped with a grin.

"I'd love for you show me around the county sometime. There's got to be fun stuff to see. How's the lake? I bet there are some interesting Civil War sites around here."

Harper felt like she was standing on a precipice, staring into the vast unknown. Did she dare take a chance on Sam? Was he different from the rest of the derelicts she'd dated? Was he different from Warner? Oh, how she wanted to believe in Sam. The two of them had a strong connection. That didn't come along everyday.

"Or maybe not," Sam said, sounding disappointed.

Sam's response was the deciding factor. She would give him a chance. Harper sat up in her seat, her voice gathering enthusiasm.

"First, the lake: It's good for fishing, but the gators tend to be unfriendly to swimmers and skiers."

Sam laughed, his mood instantly lightening. "Yeah, I can understand that."

"There's an old Civil War prison and a fort between here and Gulf

Shores that's kind of cool to see. Actually, the history here goes back further than the Civil War. I can show you where the British turned back an army of Spanish and Seminoles a hundred years before the American Revolution."

Sam cast her a sidelong glance. "You know a lot about history. Impressive," he murmured.

Heat rose in her cheeks as the distance between them shrank. Her mind replayed the deep, masculine sound of his voice and how it had reverberated through her chest, wrapping a blanket of warmth around Harper's shoulders. "I guess I'm just a dyed-in-the-wool hometown girl." It would be easy to fall for a man like Sam.

"That's a good thing."

"Thanks. I think so." Harper loved Clementine. When her cousins were stretching their wings and flying the coop, Harper sank her roots deep into the soil becoming an integral part of the town and its people. Some folks looked down on Harper for never leaving Clementine, but not Sam. He seemed to have the good grace to appreciate all that she'd accomplished. Running a successful restaurant wasn't for the fainthearted.

A lopsided grin pulled at Sam's mouth. "How about this Saturday? Do you have to be at the restaurant?"

Harper's heart leapt with anticipation. "Andi can hold down the fort," she inserted quickly. She did a mental calculation. "We can just about see the whole county in a single day, and we'll still have time to go to the beach after." It was obvious from the way Sam's muscles moved underneath his shirt that he knew his way around the gym. Getting him on the beach and having a full display of his muscles was a notion that Harper could go for.

Sam smiled broadly. "Good, it's a date."

"Yes, it is," Harper said decisively. Just because she agreed to go on a date with Sam didn't mean she was making a lifelong commitment to him. She'd take this slow and see where it led. Harper smiled a little, getting some perverse satisfaction out of knowing that Sam had asked her, not Pepper, on a date.

Pepper was about to get shown the door.

CHAPTER 4

*H*arper wasn't kidding. By noon the following Saturday, they'd seen all the sites of interest in the county and were on their way to the beach. Being co-owner of the best restaurant in the area, she wouldn't let Sam take her to another restaurant for lunch. Along with the towels, umbrella, sunscreen and blanket, she packed a scrumptious picnic lunch of chicken fingers, macaroni salad, honeydew melon and of course, mouth-watering sweet potato pie.

Sam patted his stomach, a feeling of contentment settling over him. "That was amazing. They don't make chicken like that in New Jersey." He lay down on his towel and stretched out his legs. "Good thing we brought the umbrella. I may just pass out." They'd positioned the umbrella back from them so that it offered some shade without obscuring the sun.

"Mama always said you have to wait half an hour after eating before getting in the ocean. Otherwise the crabs will get you."

He chuckled. "I'm pretty sure she meant muscle cramps."

An impish grin flitted over Harper's lips. "I was too young back then to know the difference. I thought she said crabs."

He leaned up on one elbow and looked at her, impressed that she was able to discuss her mother in such a cheerful manner. No doubt it hadn't always been that way. "I guess we'll just have to nap."

She turned her head toward him and shaded her eyes with her hand. "You know, you told me some about your Army days. What about before that?"

He lay his head back and spoke with his eyes closed. His baseball cap proudly advertising 'US Army' slid up a little as he lay on it, and some of his wavy brown hair spilled down onto the top of his forehead.

"All right, doc, what's your secret?"

"The secret behind what?" he asked lazily, appreciating how nice the warmth of the sun felt on his skin. Being out here amidst the salty breeze and breaking waves was rejuvenating.

"Behind your biceps and six-pack."

For an instant, the meaning of Harper's words didn't register. Then, a slow pleased smile stole over his lips as he sat up and looked at her. "Are my ears deceiving me, or did I just get a compliment from one Harper Boyce, a.k.a. the most eligible bachelorette in Clementine?" For Sam, working out was therapy.

Color rose in her cheeks, heightening her beauty. "Ah, I don't know about that. There are plenty of bachelorettes in Clementine more sought after than me."

"I don't believe that for a second," he countered, eyes meeting hers.

She shook her head, grinning. "You are charming." She gave him a playful shove. "Now, tell me more about your past."

He pursed his lips, collecting his thoughts. "My parents met in high school. Dad joined the Navy and went to Vietnam. He didn't see much of the enemy. He was a fueler for the jets on a carrier. When he got home, they got married. About nine and a half months later my older brother came along. Then two years after that was my turn. It was five more years before my sister decided to be born."

"Hopefully your mother had some say in that," Harper joked.

"I'm not so sure," he said straight-faced. "I heard something once about an accident they had on a weekend up in the Poconos without us kids. I checked the car. It didn't look like it'd been in any kind of an accident. I figured out they were talking about some other kind of accident and not a car wreck."

Harper giggled. "I hope they weren't disappointed."

"Oh no. They doted on her like you wouldn't believe. Between being the only girl and the last child, Claire got spoiled like there was no tomorrow. It didn't hurt her though. She turned out great. She married a dirt-poor college freshman who was flipping burgers for a living. Bart finished college, went to work for a bank and is making twice what this small-town, Southern surgeon makes. I suspect he'll retire before he's forty-five." He spoke with honest admiration, not jealousy. "I'm really proud of them both. Claire's pregnant with baby number four, and they don't show any sign of stopping."

Harper turned over to lie down on her stomach and rested her head on her crossed arms. "How come you don't have a New Jersey accent?"

"I used to, but I've lost most it from living in so many different places."

"Well," Harper said, pouring on a thick drawl, "if you stick 'round here long enough, we'll git you fixed right up and have you talking like a Southerner in no time."

"I don't doubt that," Sam said with a laugh as he lay back.

They basked in the sun, listening to the waves lazily licking the shore to the accompanying music provided by seagulls begging for scraps. Harper checked the time on her phone. "Time's up, doc. Roll over." He obeyed as she squirted sunscreen onto his back and moved her hand in lazy circles rubbing it in. His skin tingled deliciously under her touch. A reckless impulse overcame Sam. Without warning, he jumped up causing Harper to squeal in surprise. He grabbed Harper's hand and pulled her to her feet. "Come on. Let's get in the water."

"But it hasn't been half an hour yet. What about the crabs?"

He winked. "Crabs don't wear watches. They don't know what time it is." He let go of her hand and ran into the surf. She followed, jumping over waves until she was too far in to jump anymore. He grabbed her waist and held her up as he waded out.

"No! No," she screamed when she wasn't laughing and could get words out. He waded deeper until he was up to his neck. A wave washed halfway up his face as he spit out salt water. "That's what you get, meanie," she said, still laughing. He lowered her into the water as she turned to face him. In quick movements, she grabbed his shoulders and climbed onto his back.

"Crap! I think a crab has me by the toe. Your mom was right. It's too soon after eating."

She swatted his shoulder. "Stop making fun of my mama. If a crab gets you, it just serves you right." He spun around a few times as she shrieked in delight. Without warning he ducked under the water, taking her with him.

In a split second, he was above the water again, cradling her in his arms. "That was a dirty trick," Harper said, spitting out water.

"Yes, it was, but I like the way it turned out." He gazed into her eyes. Even soaking wet she was beautiful. He liked the warmth of her body against his chest, her right arm slung around his neck. She glanced back with rounded eyes.

"Look out! A wave!" she warned. He jumped high enough to lift them both over the breaking water. There was another wave right behind it that he jumped over. A deep swell took the water level down to his waist, but the wave after was taller. Sam looked at Harper and grinned, and then he dove into the wave carrying her with him. She came up sputtering.

"Samuel Wallentine, you're a menace!" she reprimanded in mock anger as she waded out of the water and walked up the sand to their spot where she toweled the water from her face and hair.

Harper certainly filled out her red tankini nicely with her sleek curves, slender arms, and shapely legs. Even without a stitch of makeup she was stunning.

Sam came out of the water to join her. He was ankle deep when three little girls, stair steps around six, four, and three-years-old ran up to him, laughing and jumping. "Mister! Throw me in!" the oldest said.

He paused and gave Harper a puzzled look, shrugging his shoulders. "Okay, if you insist." He picked up the little girl and pretended to toss her into a wave, but he didn't let go of her until she was standing in the waves, laughing hysterically. He turned to the next one, picked her up, swung back and set her down beside her sister, and then the third.

A woman had set up her umbrella and chair a few yards away from Harper. The woman called out. "Girls, stop bothering that man. Get over here and put on some sunscreen."

Immediately, all three stopped playing with Sam. "Yes, mama," they chimed and ran giggling to the umbrella where their mother began buttering them with ultraviolet protection.

A smile played on Harper's lips. Nice to know that Sam was good with kids. The day was turning out much better than Harper could've ever imagined. She'd enjoyed the intellectual stimulation between her and Sam as they discussed history while touring the Civil War sites. Now, here on the beach, it felt like heaven. Of course, it didn't hurt that Sam was a walking poster for fitness. Earlier, she'd not been able to resist making that crack about his six-pack. Sam was the kind of man a girl could wait a lifetime for. And for some inexplicable reason, Sam was interested in her!

Her pulse quickened as Sam strode toward her.

He plopped down on his towel in the shade of the beach umbrella. When he reclined onto his back, his hand brushed Harper's. A current of awareness raced through her.

"Sorry," he said absently, withdrawing his hand and draping it over his stomach.

The temptation to be close to Sam was too strong to ignore. In a swift movement, she reached over and clasped his hand. "I don't mind," she said peering into his arresting jade eyes. Harper wanted Sam to see her with those eyes, often and deeply. She pulled his hand to her lips and kissed his knuckles. The corners of his mouth curled up. She could tell his mind was churning and hoped it was churning in a good way. Hadn't she just told herself that morning that she wasn't ready for another relationship? And yet, here she was initiating one. Maybe that was her problem—always throwing caution to the wind.

Sam didn't say anything for a few minutes. The little girls ran past shrieking to chase a flock of gulls that had landed several yards away. Harper's nerves ate away at her. Had she taken things too far? Moved too fast? Sam was the sensible one. It wasn't smart to get involved with the town doctor. If things went sideways, it wasn't like Harper could just show Sam the door like she had Warner. Sam was here for the long term. They would be forced to see each other often. With a heavy pit in her stomach, Harper started to withdraw her hand, but Sam gripped it, preventing her from pulling away.

"I like this," he said simply as he angled to face her.

Just like that, her fears dissolved.

A warm sensation washed over her from head to toe, and it wasn't the ocean breeze wafting along the sun-heated sand. A surge of electricity buzzed through her veins as Sam leaned in. There was a smoldering light simmering in his gold-flecked eyes that kindled a fire inside of Harper. When his lips touched hers, she met him full force, drinking in his intoxicating sweetness that sent an aching need through her. He took the hand that had held hers and put it behind her back, pulling her close. He deepened the kiss, a hot flame scorching through her, melting her insides. No one had ever kissed her this way before, so completely and thoroughly, lighting her every cell on fire.

It went through Harper's mind that she was falling hard and fast. It was too soon. Fear streaked through her. She didn't want to get hurt again. Could she trust Sam with her heart? They were just getting to know each other. Yet, it felt like they'd known each other forever. Was Sam the one? Had Harper finally found her man?

"Ewwwww!" a voice behind them screeched. Three little giggles resounded from the girls who had returned from defending the beach against seagulls.

Harper buried her face in Sam's chest for a moment, but she couldn't hide from the little faces watching. She pushed back and did a brush-off wave. "Okay girls, go build a sand castle or find some clams or something." They ran off, giggling.

Harper looked back at Sam who wore the smug expression of one who knew he was all that. "That was amazing," he murmured, stroking her cheek with his thumb.

Heat fanned her cheeks. "It was all right," she said casually with a wink. "You're not a bad kisser."

His eyebrow shot up. "Not bad, huh?" Amusement twinkled in the depths of his arresting eyes. "Maybe we should try again." His lips brushed against hers, sending delicious tingles circling down her spine.

She blushed thinking of the little girls nearby and the girls' mother. "I need to cool off. Come on." She sprang to her feet and took his hand as they ran toward the water. This time, Sam didn't pick her up and throw her. He seemed more concerned, or gentle, or something. It didn't bother Harper at all.

Before long, the sun neared the end of its downward arc toward the ocean, stretching golden veins over the water. "I guess we'd better get going," Sam said.

Harper sighed. "I guess so. I don't want today to end."

He brightened like he'd just had a revolutionary idea. "We can continue it tomorrow."

Harper's heart leapt as she laughed. "Yes, we can."

Sam caressed her with his eyes. "And the day after."

Harper touched his hair, her finger linking around a strand. "And, so on."

Sam encircled her waist, bringing her close. "I like the way you think." His lips took hers in another long, intoxicating kiss that sent her swirling to the sky above.

A few minutes later, they walked over to their towels and folded them up, packed the items from their picnic, and collapsed the umbrella. They managed to each get everything in one of their arms, so they could walk hand in hand back to the car.

Conversation drifted easily between them on the drive back to Clementine. Harper enjoyed the feel of Sam's strong fingers around hers. Despite the fact that they were moving into uncharted territory, Harper felt good about what the future held. Sam felt her gaze and smiled. Things had certainly evolved in an unexpected and good direction.

Time to put the hurts of the past behind her and move forward with a wonderful, intelligent man. Harper had always pegged doctors to be analytical and on the boring side. She grinned, thinking nothing could be farther from the truth.

Sam Wallentine had lit her world on fire, and Harper had a feeling this was only the beginning.

CHAPTER 5

*D*ouglas Foster looked uncomfortable on the exam table. He teetered a little as he sat holding onto the sides. Sam wheeled his exam stool over to the computer and sat down to enter Douglas's symptoms.

"How long has this been going on?" he asked.

"Started five or six years ago, but it would come on for a week or maybe a month and go away for months, and then happen all over again. Now it's been steady for four months and getting pretty annoying."

Sam grinned. It seemed a lot of things were annoying to Douglas. Sam wondered why Douglas didn't mention the rash on his first visit when he'd asked to have his lungs checked. Then again, Douglas had probably been testing the water on the first go-around to see if he could trust Sam before coming to him about a true ailment."What's it doing to you?" Now that Sam and Harper were together, Sam had an added interest in Douglas.

Douglas rolled up his sleeves. He usually wore a blue mechanic's suit around town, and today was no exception. "To start with, there's this rash. It's the worst on my arms. Really itches and burns." There was a dry, red, scaling eruption on both arms from the backs of his hands up to the middle of his biceps.

"Sure enough. Have you been putting anything on it?"

"My granddaughter, you know Harper, has been smearing this aloe sunburn kind of stuff on it. I tried petroleum jelly. It works just as well and is a whole lot cheaper."

Sam lost his train of thought for a second. The way Douglas looked at him let Sam know that Douglas knew he and Harper were a couple. Sam wondered if Douglas approved of him. He was tempted to open up a conversation but thought better of it. Better to keep things professional at work.

"Does the rash come up anyplace else?"

"Nope. I'd have thought that something from the sun would have been on my neck and my head, but it isn't. Also, there's this." He unbuttoned his shirt. "I hurt all up and down on my ribs." Sam felt along the edge of his breastbone where the ribs intersected it.

"Do you ever get swollen here?"

"Nope." No elaboration. Just a one-word answer.

Sam examined Douglas's chest, front and back, his belly, and his neck. "You've got some costochondritis going on ... inflammation of the cartilage in the ribcage," he explained when he saw Douglas's blank expression. "I'll write you a prescription to take for it. It should be gone within a few days. I'll give you a lotion to put on your arms too and see if we can get rid of that rash."

"What is it?" Douglas asked.

"It's a pretty routine dermatitis. Well, I say routine. It's routine for us. I know it's not routine for you. It's nothing to worry about."

Douglas grunted. He took the prescriptions and left.

Sam finished typing up his note and walked out to the front desk. Felicia and Jan sat chatting. "Mr. Foster was cheerful as ever, wasn't he?"

The ladies giggled. "He's just a ray of sunshine. That's the last patient of the morning. You can break for lunch."

"Sounds good to me." Sam walked back to his office and pulled out his dermatology atlas. He flipped through page after page of rashes. They all looked the same. Oh, well. He'd just have to give the rash time to clear up. If it didn't, he could always take a biopsy and send it over to the lab at the hospital.

"Doc! Doc! Come up here," Jan called.

He walked to the front. Both women sat behind the front desk, looking upset. Jan pointed out the front window. He noticed they hadn't walked closer to the window.

Outside, two men strolled down the sidewalk on the other side of the street. He didn't recognize them, but there were still plenty of people in town whom he wouldn't recognize. They both wore pullover shirts, jeans with holes in them, and running shoes. The older one was on the portly side. The younger was tall and skinny with a ragged beard. Both men had shaggy hair like they'd cut it them-selves without using a mirror. They didn't seem to be in much of a hurry.

"Who are they?"

Felicia answered. "The younger, taller one with the beard is Judd Barber."

"I didn't realize that he'd been let out of prison," Jan said with a note of concern.

Felicia picked back up on the narrative. Her voice was hushed in disapproval. "Judd robbed a bank over in Fairhope and killed a customer in the process. The judge gave him ten years for the robbery and only one for killing the lady. Her kids are teenagers now."

Sam made a face. "Why only one year?"

"Judd claimed that on his way into the back of the bank, the door knocked his gun out of his hand, and it went off. The woman just happened to be standing in the wrong place." Her voice hardened. "That poor woman's just as dead as if Judd held the gun up to her and pulled the trigger. But his lawyer managed to convince the jury that it was an accident."

"Wow. What about the other guy?"

"Peter Morrison. I actually went on a date with him in high school." Felicia shuddered. "That was downright scary. He's just plain crazy. There's no nicer way to say it. He's been locked up on and off through the years. Latest thing was shooting out the streetlights. Since he had such a record, and he was a felon with a handgun, he got five years. Looks like they're both out of jail and are re-connecting."

"Birds of a feather flock together," Jan added sourly.

They watched the duo walk down the sidewalk. The men paused to rattle the speed limit sign. It held its position in spite of their attempt at broad daylight vandalism. They'd only taken a few more steps when a deputy car pulled up next to them and stopped at the curb. Jim Wilson got out and walked around his car to the men. From what Sam could tell, he seemed like a dedicated lawman but like many in his profession, had a severe case of doughnut poisoning around his middle. The two men on the sidewalk paused for a moment. Peter Morrison smiled, reaching out and poking Jim's protruding belly. Jim gave the finger an irritated brush-off.

"Doesn't look like they've learned how to behave civilly," Felicia observed. Sam crossed the office lobby to get closer to the window. Jim motioned to his car, but the men waved in a gesture declining his offer. "Looks like Jim was offering them a ride, hopefully all the way to the county line," Felicia added.

"Sounds like those two aren't real popular," Sam observed.

"They're probably the sorriest people ever to come out of Clementine," Jan said. "I don't have to take a poll to know that everybody wishes they wouldn't have come back, I promise you that."

"I'll have to keep my eyes open," Sam said. They watched as the men turned their backs on Deputy Jim Wilson and walked toward The Magnolia. Sam tensed. If they went inside the restaurant, he was going too. No way was he leaving Harper alone to deal with those hooligans. Jim called after them, shook his head, and again gestured toward the back seat of his car. This time, he was more insistent. They complied and climbed into the car. Jim drove them around the corner and out of sight.

Felicia shuddered. "Jim's a brave guy. I wouldn't be caught alone in a car with those two."

"Oh, I'm sure he's had to deal with worse people," Sam said.

"I doubt that," Felicia countered, and Sam could tell from the intensity in her voice that she meant it.

CHAPTER 6

Sam and Harper kept seeing each other through the summer. A few of Clementine's old maids had predicted this the moment Sam came to town and opened his medical practice. It turned out that Sam and Harper both liked bowling but didn't get to do that more than once or twice a month, because they had to go all the way to Dothan or up to Montgomery to find a bowling alley.

Most of the time, they took long walks along the many wooded paths that carved the lush landscape of Clementine and went to the beach as often as possible. Many evenings, after The Magnolia had closed, Sam found himself at Harper's house where she whipped up a gourmet supper for them both.

Sam had been worried about how he would adjust to civilian life. As it turned out, it was much easier than he thought, primarily because of Harper.

Summer was galloping into the history books, but here along the coast, the warm weather persisted into fall and sometimes past the first day of winter. Sam didn't hide his admiration for Harper, but he knew better than to say it too often. She clearly liked being with him as much as he did her, but she modestly turned away compliments. Besides, she was an independent business woman. She didn't need a guy fawning over her to make her feel confident. Sam respected that. He longed to take their relationship to the next level but sensed that Harper was reluctant to do so. He'd broached the topic a couple times in an offhand way with comments such as, "My house is starting to feel lonely with me wandering around in my boxers."

"Now, that's a sight I'd like to see," Harper had joked before changing the subject. Sam knew that Harper was gun-shy about making a lifelong commitment because of her past experiences with men. He hoped that as time went on Harper would realize what he already knew—that the two of them were a great fit. Sam knew this in some instinctive way he couldn't define. The more time he spent around Harper, the more he craved her presence. Sam hardly knew what to do with himself without Harper.

On the last day of August, the office schedule had a gap at the end of the morning, followed by the thirty-minute lunch break. "Come on y'all," Felicia said, "let's head over to The Magnolia for lunch. My treat."

"Don't you think people will talk if we're out together?" Jan teased.

"Oh, please. We're both old enough to be his mother," Felicia retorted.

Jan cut her eyes at Felicia. "Maybe you are." They both laughed, knowing that if anyone could pass for Sam's mother it would be Jan, the oldest.

"You're more like my big sisters," Sam offered.

Felicia clucked her tongue. "We have to watch this one. He's a silver-tongued devil."

They walked to the restaurant kitty corner across the intersection at the end of the block. Andi greeted them at the hostess stand. "Hiya, folks. Nice to see y'all." Her hand went to her hip as she tipped her head, pursing her lips. "I have a question."

"Shoot," Felicia said.

"If you're here and someone gets sick over at the office, who's gonna take care of them?"

Jan was the first to speak. "We put up a sign that says we're out to lunch." She sounded a little put-out that Andi would ask such a thing.

"We'll watch the office from here," Felicia said. "That way, if anyone should have an emergency, we can see them knocking on the door."

Andi shrugged. "Sounds good. I just wondered. All right, follow me." She gestured toward a table by the window that faced the street.

They'd just gotten seated when Harper emerged from the kitchen, wiping her hands on her apron. When she saw Sam, her face lit up, a wide smile curving her lips as she came toward them.

Heat sparked through Sam as he rose to his feet. "Hey, beautiful." He bridged the distance between them and caught Harper around the waist, giving her a quick peck on the lips. Something tender settled into her eyes.

"Hey, you," she said softly. Time seemed to slow as Sam and Harper locked gazes.

Jan cleared her throat, prompting them to pull apart. Color rose in Harper's cheeks as she stepped back and glanced around at the customers who were watching their every move.

Sam spread his hands. "We'd might as well own it. Everyone knows we're a couple."

Harper laughed, her shoulders relaxing. "Yes, I suppose you're right. It's official, folks," she proclaimed loudly. "The doc and I are officially a couple."

"I'm just glad you turkeys are finally admitting it," Felicia said tartly with a large smile.

Sam slipped his arm around Harper's waist, pulling her close. He couldn't be more pleased that they were openly proclaiming their affection. One step closer to his goal of winning Harper's heart.

"This is a nice surprise," Harper said. "What're y'all doing here?"

Jan smiled brightly. "We had some extra time to come out for lunch, so here we are."

"Glad to see we won out over the Dixie Freeze." Harper flashed a cheeky grin.

Marie walked up and stood beside Harper. "Hi, gang. What can we get for you?" She took their drink and food orders at the same time.

"I'll have a diet coke and the pork chop platter," Jan said.

Felicia spoke next. "I'd like a regular Coke and a mushroom Swiss burger with onion rings, please."

Harper turned to Sam, her eyes glittering with mischief. "And grilled cheese for you, sir?"

"How about the Philly Cheesesteak with fries on the side?" He leaned in close and whispered in Harper's ear. "I'll save the grilled cheese for later tonight when I come over. Maybe I can have it as an appetizer before the main dish." He pumped his eyebrows, relishing the deep flush that fanned Harper's cheeks. Harper shook her head, giving Sam a reproving look, but her eyes were soft and glowing.

Marie took the order into the kitchen. Harper and Sam sat down at the table with his staff. "I can only stay for a couple of minutes," Harper began. "It's the lunch rush, as you know. Nearly every seat is taken."

Jan glanced around the room. "I know most of the customers." She nodded to a couple of tables across the room. "Tourists?"

"Kind of," Harper said. "Two sisters and their families from Missouri. They're headed down to Pensacola to see their son in the Air Force."

"Nice. They just pulled off the Interstate and walked in?"

Harper shook her head. "No. Turns out, word of The Magnolia has made it all the way to Odessa, MO. Who'd a thunk?"

"I'm not the least bit surprised," Sam said. This earned him an appreciative smile from Harper.

"Harper, how do you like Sam's new house?" Jan asked.

Sam had settled on a one-story brick home on the west side of town that gave him easy access to the county highway leading to the hospital in Daphne yet still close to Clementine and the office. And, of course, to Harper.

"Cozy. It's definitely not as cushy as the mansions at Hudson Bay, but it's perfect for Sam." Harper's eye caught Sam's as they shared a smile.

"I love it," Sam interjected. "I never thought I'd have a hundred acres of land, but here we are. I've got a timber company coming out to look at deforesting most of the land. They'll pay for a stand of yellow pine, maintain it, and in sixteen years come back to harvest and put in new trees. It makes the land pay for itself. Up by the house, I put in a big garden. Eventually, I'll plant some fruit trees and who knows what else. Maybe I'll even run a few cows in the pasture."

"Quite a deal," Felicia said. "And you used Pepper for your realtor, right?"

Sam chuckled. "Yes. Pepper was disappointed with my choice. The house is nothing fancy, and Pepper thought I should be a high-society golfer not a pretend farmer. One day when I have a family, I'll build a bigger house, probably on the back of the property by the river, but for now this is more than enough." He glanced at Harper whose face had turned red. Sam wondered if it was because he'd mentioned one day having a family. Harper had to know that he was referring to her and the family he hoped they'd have. His stomach tightened. Would Harper ever be ready to settle down?

Felicia clucked her tongue. "Good old Pepper. I'm sure she was looking for more than just a sale. Sam, you need to be careful of that one. Everybody knows she's on the hunt."

Jan put in her two-cent's worth. "I'm not sure whether Pepper figures those kids of hers need a male influence around, or she's just getting tired of them. I hope it's not the latter. But she chases every single man who passes through this place and some of the non-single ones too, bless her heart."

Harper said nothing. Sam sensed she was uncomfortable. He wished he could read her thoughts.

The conversation drifted to another topic as Felicia turned to Harper. "Did you hear that those good-for-nothing criminals Peter Morrison and Judd Barber are back in town?"

Harper nodded. "Sure did. They stopped in here and asked for some pie."

Jan looked mortified. "Did you give them any?"

"Of course," Harper said matter-of-factly. "I'm not gonna turn a hobo away hungry. At the same time, I'm not going to be their personal pantry either. I gave them a good meal and sent them on their way, but I also told them it was a one-time deal."

"Good for you," Felicia said with an approving nod. "That was the Christian thing to do."

A second later, she switched gears. "You know, the county fair's coming up in a week and a half." There was a wicked glint in her eyes. "Doc, you got a date yet?"

Sam feigned naivety. "A date? For the fair? I didn't know that was a thing." He looked at Harper who was watching him with an amused expression.

Jan didn't seem to realize Sam was being sarcastic. "Oh yeah. It's a big thing. That's where anyone who's anyone goes to be seen. We're sponsoring the cake walk this year."

Sam's eyes widened. "We are?" He could tell Harper was trying hard not to laugh.

Jan rolled her eyes. "While I appreciate that you trust us to do your marketing, you really should know what's going on. Don't they have county fairs in New Jersey?"

Sam thought for a minute. "Well, yeah, but they're mostly for farmers and 4-H kids to show off their work." He held up a finger. "Oh, and for kids to go on worn-out rides that put their lives in danger. They aren't really social events up there."

"Around here they're the biggest deal of the year." Jan made a point of looking at Harper. "You'd better get a date and fast before everyone's taken."

"I'm sponsoring the dunking booth," Harper announced. "The money's going to the women's auxiliary's charity work." She stood up from her chair. "It was nice talking with y'all, but I'd better get back to work."

Sam was no dummy. He knew he needed to strike while the iron was hot. He grabbed Harper's hand, tugging her back toward him. "Will you go to the fair with me?"

Harper pursed her lips like she was debating a large decision. "Well, since we did just announce to the world that we're a couple ..."

Sam grinned broadly. "Yes, we did," he said with a touch of pride.

"And," Harper continued, "since you asked nicely." She winked at Felicia and Jan. "I suppose the answer is *yes*."

Felicia and Jan gave one another victorious looks. Sam grinned inwardly. Next, his staff would be taking credit for getting him and Harper together. There's no way Sam would've gone to the fair without Harper. Asking her had been a formality.

Harper's expression took on a new light. "You'll get to meet my cousin Scarlett and her husband."

"Oh yeah?" Sam looked forward to meeting more of Harper's family. He knew how close Harper was to Scarlett. It would be good to finally put a face with the person he'd heard so much about.

"Harper, where's your and Scarlett's other restaurant located?" Felicia asked.

"Helen, Georgia."

"Scarlett's married to Rocket Breeland," Jan gushed. "He's the starting quarterback for The Georgia Patriots."

"I heard something about that." Sam winked and flashed a cavalier grin at Harper. "It's a date. I'm taking you to the fair."

"Just as you should," Jan said primly. "You'll need to pick her up early."

"Oh, and wear something comfortable," Felicia admonished.

"But nice," Jan added.

Sam looked at Harper. The corners of her mouth quivered. Sam had to bite back his own chortle. Their eyes met for one long, delicious moment. "See you tonight?" she asked.

The hint of promise in Harper's deep blue eyes sent a thrill racing through Sam's veins. "Yes, ma'am. I wouldn't miss it for the world."

Harper smiled at Felicia and Jan. "Thank you, ladies," she mouthed as she turned and sauntered away, her glossy hair bouncing on her shoulders with every graceful step.

"She's the cream of the crop," Felicia said, her chin jiggling as she squared her jaw.

Jan gave Sam a pointed look. "You'd better hold onto her."

"Don't worry. I intend to," Sam said, the conviction of his words ringing in his ears.

CHAPTER 7

Sam needed something huge. A grand gesture that would let Harper know he was serious about moving things forward. He'd learned the hard way in the blistering, unforgiving Afghan desert that there were no guarantees in life. How many times had he looked at Sergeant Mirabelle and promised himself that he'd ask her out on a date the following day? In the time it took to draw in a single breath, all of the hopes and dreams for Mirabelle's future, along with the other ill-fated members of his medical team, vanished in a cloud of acrid smoke.

This thing with Harper was the real deal. Sam wanted to build a life with her. No, it was more than that. Sam needed Harper in his life. He understood Harper's reticence to get serious. She'd been hurt before. He grunted. *Who hasn't?* Sam had certainly had his share of heartache. The only thing anybody could do was move past it and keep on going. For a while after the explosion, Sam experienced survivor guilt, wondering why he'd been lucky enough to live when others with spouses and children hadn't.

As time went on, Sam's perspective was starting to shift. Maybe it was being here in Clementine, surrounded by salt-of-the-earth people who truly cared about one another. Sam saw each day as a gift, realizing that no one was guaranteed a tomorrow. No longer would Sam sit back and wait for the good things in life to come his way. He planned to go after those things ... starting with what he wanted most —Harper.

After work, he ran to the local florist and bought a large bouquet of flowers. With a sparkle in her eye, Cindy Stubblefield handed Sam the bouquet. "I threw in a few extra calla lilies because I know those are Harper's favorite. Be sure and tell her I said hello."

Sam chuckled, inwardly pleased that news of his and Harper's couple status was getting through the grapevine. "I'm learning that there aren't any secrets in Clementine."

Cindy laughed. "No, siree. There aren't." She winked. "I knew you were a fast learner."

With a spring in his step, Sam went up the walk to Harper's door, hardly noticing the tenderness in his knees. Holding the flowers in front of him, he punched the doorbell. A few seconds later, Harper opened the door. Her eyes popped in surprise when she saw the flowers.

"For you, madam," he said with a slight bow.

"Thank you." She reached for them and brought them to her nose. "They smell wonderful." She stepped back. "Come on in. You're full of surprises today. First, you stop into The Magnolia for lunch and now these." She looked at the flowers, and then back up at him, an appreciative smile curving her lips. "Thank you," she said softly.

Harper had changed into jeans and a form-fitting red t-shirt that rounded out her slim curves nicely. Sam closed the door and stepped up to Harper. His gaze took in her heart-shaped face with its delicate features before settling on her delectable lips. "I've been thinking about you all day," he murmured as he encircled her waist and drew her to him. Harper held out the flowers so they wouldn't get crushed.

Harper grunted softly in surprise, a slight smile touching her lips. "You're in rare form."

Her expression, everything about her, was so alive that it surged adrenaline through his veins. With deliberate gentleness, he caressed the curve of her cheek, appreciating the smoothness of her milky skin. His fingers moved to her mouth as he traced the outline of her wonderful lips. She tipped her head back. With a sigh, her lips parted, her eyes deepening with an intensity that matched his own fevered need for her.

He removed the flowers from her hand and placed them on the foyer table. In a swift movement, he angled her toward the wall and pushed her against it. Her hands went around his neck as she pulled him closer.

His lips came down on hers. Sam kissed her long and hard, holding nothing back. No wilting violet, Harper's passion met his own, sending them tumbling into fiery flames of harmony. Sam marveled at how someone so petite and dainty could have the power to move him so.

Finally, Harper put the flats of her palms to his chest and pushed back enough to be able to look at him. Ever so slowly, she smiled. "You're pretty good at that."

His eyes moved over her face, absorbing every detail. "It just keeps getting better and better."

"Yes, it does," she said, her voice husky.

Sam had intended to wait until after they'd eaten to move into the serious phase of the conversation, but the urgency of everything he wanted to say rose inside him, demanding to be released.

Harper glanced at the flowers. "I guess I should put those in some water."

Not ready to let her go, Sam held her fast. Harper's eyes lit with a faint amusement as she tilted her head. "What?"

"I love you." There it was. He loved her. All day, Sam had tried to pinpoint the precise moment when he fell in love with Harper. Finally, he realized that it must've been from the moment he saw her … or at least from the night she first cooked dinner for him. Time seemed to halt in its tracks, and he realized he was holding his breath, waiting for her response.

His gut tightened when hesitation crept into her eyes. A ball of confusion swirled inside him. Had Harper not just felt what he had? What Sam and Harper had didn't come along everyday. This was rare, something to be cherished. The words tumbled out of their own accord. "I want to build a life with you."

"Sam," she began. "I care about you deeply."

"But?" Her tight expression shot daggers through his heart.

"Shouldn't we give it more time?"

Sam tried to digest the meaning of Harper's words. "Are you saying that you want us to have a future together?" There was a slight pause before Harper spoke, but for Sam, it seemed like her silence stretched on for an eternity. He was hurt, conflicted.

Harper offered a tight smile. "I care about you, Sam, I really do."

"Okay, then what's the problem?" He could hear the hardness in his own voice.

"I've just been hurt before … I want to make sure that this is right."

Her comment was a slap in the face. "So, you don't trust me?"

Her eyes rounded. "No, it's not that at all," she said quickly. "It's just that with Warner, I thought everything was going great, and then, Bam! It all exploded in my face. I just want to be sure, that's all." Her voice dribbled off.

"I'm not Warner," he said stiffly, stepping away from her.

She caught his arm. "I know that." Her voice rose, and there was a hint of anxiety in her eyes. "It's just that—"

Sam clenched his jaw. "Quite frankly, it hurts that you would lump me in with the Warners of the world. I don't group you with my past failed relationships."

Her face fell. "That's not what I'm doing. I'm just trying to be practical about this. I don't have the luxury of being wrong about you."

He rocked back. "What's that supposed to mean?"

She sucked in a hard breath, running her hands through her hair. "You live in Clementine. If things don't work out between us. Well, it could be awkward."

He pushed out a hard laugh. "So, you think we're doomed for failure, is that it?"

"No," she blurted. Moisture rose in her eyes. "I just want us to be cautious. That's all." She searched his face. "Sam, I care about you." Her voice quivered. "More than I've ever cared about anyone before."

He blinked, processing her words. Harper cared. His heart lightened.

"I want us to see where this goes. I just don't wanna move too fast."

This was not how Sam had planned for this evening to go. Then again, what did he expect? He knew that Harper carried some deep wounds. Also, everyone processed situations differently. Two people could go through the same exact experience and come out reacting differently. Some people suffered more from PTSD than others. Maybe he shouldn't fault Harper for being afraid.

Harper touched his cheek, cradling it in her palm. "Don't give up on me, okay?"

The pleading in her deep blue eyes helped ease the sting from her reluctance to move forward as quickly as he desired. "Okay." His shoulders relaxed.

She stepped close and slipped her arms around his neck. Her mouth moved against his, soft and imploring. Everything in Sam wanted to melt into her, losing himself in her touch. But there was the slightest part of him that held back, questioning if the kiss was forced, like Harper was trying too hard.

A few minutes later, Harper pulled back, searching his face. "Can I make you that grilled cheese sandwich?"

Sam was still smarting from Harper's words, but he wanted her body and soul. He wanted her to love him as he loved her—all in, holding nothing back. "Sure," he heard himself say. "Don't think I don't know what you're doing," he grumbled.

"What's that?" she asked innocently, reaching for the flowers.

Her lashes swept over her cheekbones in such a feminine motion that it sent Sam's pulse skittering. "You're trying to feed me to get your way." He felt pouty and irritable.

Her velvety laughter rippled through the air. "Why Sam Wallentine, I'd never dream of doing anything of the sort," she said, slathering on a thick Southern Belle voice. She motioned with her head. "This way, sir," she chirped.

He followed her, watching the gentle swaying of her hips. "I feel like I'm being led by the Pied Piper," he said dryly.

Harper just laughed. She knew exactly what she was doing, and it was working. Her fluid hair swished jauntily on her erect shoulders. This woman had a hold on him like no other woman had before. In other words, Sam was a goner. The question Sam had to ask himself was—how long was he willing to wait for Harper to come around? Would she eventually come around, or would they always be stuck here in the wasteland of her relationship PTSD? Before coming here tonight, Sam had felt so certain about the future and everything it held.

Now, everything was muddy.

CHAPTER 8

*T*hat weekend, the fair arrived. A closed sign hung on the front door of The Magnolia. Sam picked Harper up at her home, and they drove to the fairground. Harper bubbled with excitement, reminding Sam of a kid on Christmas Eve. Her enthusiasm was infectious as he grinned.

"What should I expect of the fair?"

Her smile was a mile wide as she shifted in her seat with a slight hop. "Probably a lot of the same stuff you're used to: kiddie rides, cotton candy, deep fried butter, the dunking booth ..."

"Wait, wait," he interrupted. "Did you say deep fried butter?" He shot her an incredulous look. "Do you know what that could do to a person's coronary arteries?"

A hearty laugh rumbled in her throat. "I can only imagine. They say it's like drinking a glass of melted grease."

"That's exactly what it is."

"And that's to say nothing about the deep-fried candy bars, cupcakes, and cheese sticks."

"Oh, I'm shutting this place down. I've got to protect my patients from that garbage. Deep fried cupcakes?"

"Battered and cooked in lard." She gave him a chastising look. "Don't you dare shut it down. It's tradition," she said proudly.

"Yeah, and for a long time so was witch-burning."

"Ha ha, funny guy," she said dryly, but he could tell from the smile tugging at her lips that she was amused.

"What about the dunking booth? Didn't you say The Magnolia's sponsoring that one?"

"Sure did. We're putting local celebrities up there for it. So far I've got the mayor, the high school principal, and a weatherman from the TV station in Montgomery. He's going to broadcast from the fair too. It'll give us some good publicity. You know," she mused, "I still have room for a couple more people on the dunking seat." He could feel her eyes studying him. "I bet a lot of people would love to dunk their doctor. After everything you do to them, it'd be a little payback." There was a hint of vindication in her voice.

He pulled his eyes off the road and glanced at her. She pumped her eyebrows in an exaggerated manner, making her look adorable.

A smile slid over his lips as he tightened his hold on the steering wheel. "You make me sound like I'm torturing patients instead of treating them."

"I plead the fifth," she joked. A second later, she caught hold of his arm, leaning close to him. "Whaddaya say, doc? Are you game for the dunking seat?"

He caught a whiff of the fruity scent of her shampoo, her hair tickling his skin. The sparkle in her eyes combined with her zest was enough to make him agree to almost anything, but Harper didn't know that. He pursed his lips. "I might be persuaded. If ..."

"If what?" she asked in amusement.

"A week's worth of grilled cheese sandwiches, for starters."

"For starters, huh? What else?" She slid her hand around his neck, linking her fingers through his hair. Her touch sent sparks through him.

"A back and neck massage."

She rubbed her hand over his shoulders, massaging them. "My

pleasure," she murmured in a sultry tone. She leaned over and whispered in his ear. "Do we have a deal?"

Her warm breath tickled his ear, sending tingles rippling through him. "Deal," he said with gusto.

"Awesome," she said triumphantly. "Aside from the personal perks, you'll be happy to know the money goes to support the Women's Auxiliary Service League. This will be good for your practice. People see you as the guy in the white coat. This will show that you have a human side too."

"Nah, I'm just a medical robot." He lifted one hand off the steering wheel and sliced it through the air woodenly.

She laughed. "A hunky, charming robot who's an adequate kisser … with an insatiable appetite for grilled cheese sandwiches."

He pulled a frown. "Adequate kisser, huh? I'll show you some kissing later that will curl your toes."

She grinned. "I'll hold you to that." She squeezed his biceps. "Nice," she drawled.

He shook his head, chuckling; but truthfully, he appreciated the compliment. After their tense conversation a few days prior, Sam worried that things might get weird between them. However, that hadn't been the case. If anything, things had gotten better since the hard conversation. Harper rested her head on his shoulder. The two of them fit so well together. Surely Harper could see that.

When they reached the fairground entrance, Sam pulled up to the orange traffic cones and rolled down his window. Harper reached across him and handed the attendant a sponsor's pass.

The attendant pointed. "All the way to the end of this row, turn left, and park in the row before the entrance," he said as he handed it back.

Sam looked at Harper. "Impressive. You didn't tell me I was bringing a VIP."

"Hmph. There are still plenty of things you don't know about me," she replied.

They drove to the VIP area where Harper handed the pass out Sam's window again. A smiling deputy opened the rope, which kept commoners out of the private parking area. "There you go, folks. Park anywhere. Enjoy the show."

Sam nodded. "Thanks, Oscar. How's the blood sugar doing?"

"Pretty good, doc. Next time my wife's in there, why don't you tell her to take it easy on the pies and cookies? I ain't got no self-control, so she's gotta help me."

"You've got it. I'll see what I can do."

The deputy handed back the pass. "Leave this on your windshield." He looked into the car, a wide grin breaking over his face. "Oh, hey, Harper. I heard you two was an item."

"Are we?" She gave Sam a befuddled look. "We're a couple?" she asked in a confused tone, but there was a glint of laughter in her eyes.

Sam played along with a deadpan expression. "Do you actually think I'd get hooked up with this woman?"

There was an awkward pause as color blotched into the deputy's cheeks. "Well, you know how people spread rumors around here. There's just not that much to talk about except each other."

Sam felt kind of bad for yanking Oscar's chain.

Harper laughed, slipping an arm through Sam's. "I'm just teasing. We are a couple."

"You got me," Oscar said with a good-natured grin. "Enjoy the fair." He tipped his hat and held the rope while Sam pulled into the small lot and found a parking space. Sam bounded around the car and opened Harper's door.

They had just started walking toward the gate when a motor roared behind them. Oscar called out cheerfully, "Hey there, Rocket. Miss Scarlett. I mean Mrs. Scarlett. Welcome back." He stood back with the rope in his hand and waved them into the parking area. "Just find an empty spot and it's yours."

"Oh good! It's my cousin," Harper exclaimed. She grabbed Sam's hand. "Come on. I can't wait for you to meet her." They watched the Porsche park and Harper ran over, dragging Sam with her.

The passenger door opened. A stunning brunette unfolded, flashing a warm smile.

"Harper! Hey! How're you doing?" she said, embracing Harper in a tight hug.

On the other side, a super-fit man nimbly climbed out of the driver's side of the supercharged sports car. He walked around to Harper and held out his arms for a hug. A second later, he pulled back. "Hey, Harper. Who's your friend?"

Harper did the introductions. "Rigby Breeland, Scarlett, this is Dr. Sam Wallentine. He's our new town doc since Vernie, um, had to leave." Sam could tell Harper's words were heavy with underlying meaning. Sam had heard quite a bit about Vernon from Jan and Felicia. He searched his brain. Vernon had been involved with Scarlett. There was some sort of uproar involving Douglas Foster. It came to him in a flash. Douglas had wanted to sue Rigby for causing him injury as he rescued him from his burning home. In the end, it was discovered that Vernon was the instigator, trying to get Rigby out of the way so he could win Scarlett.

Sam grinned inwardly. He'd feared that after military life Clementine would be sleepy and dull. Nothing was farther from the truth. Sam was becoming engrossed in this town, and it didn't hurt that he was dating the most fascinating woman he'd ever met.

The fair was impressive for such a small town. It focused on the local peanut and cotton crops, but the livestock barns were completely full of animals, their proud owners vying for first place. Harper slipped her hand into Sam's. Warmth flowed through his chest when he felt her tiny grip, which was surprisingly strong. He looked at her. She was smiling up at him.

"What do they have to eat here that I can't get in New Jersey?" Sam asked. "And I don't want any fried butter or chocolate bars."

"Corn dogs?" asked Rigby.

"Nope. Got those."

"Gulf shrimp on a stick," offered Scarlett.

"Like scampi? Had it before." Sam hadn't really known what to expect from Rigby and Scarlett, especially after hearing so much about them. The two were surprisingly down-to-earth and fun to be around. Harper and Scarlett were super close, which was to be expected since they were doubly connected—cousins and business partners.

"How about hushpuppies?" Harper suggested.

Sam made a face. "You mean the shoes?"

Looks passed between Harper, Scarlett, and Rigby as they laughed. "No, Yankee boy, I mean deep fried corn bread batter with bits of onion in it," Harper retorted.

"Sounds interesting," Sam mused. "Let's try it."

Rigby led the way to the food area. The crowd parted as Rigby came through. A few people actually applauded but most just smiled and waved. Boys held out their hands for high fives. Rigby took it all in stride with a gracious manner, which was impressive. Being the only doctor in Clementine was enough notoriety for Sam who already felt like he was under the microscope. He couldn't imagine being a star NFL player.

When the last of the hushpuppies were eaten, Sam wiped his fingers on a napkin. "I've been missing out all my life. Those were fantastic."

"You'd better believe it," Harper said, glancing at her phone. "Okay, doc. You're due at the dunking booth in fifteen minutes. Ready?"

Rigby smacked him on the back. "Dunking booth? Really, Sam? Good for you."

Scarlett laughed. "Rigby's just glad he's not on the hot seat."

"Amen to that," Rigby said.

"Be sure and stay clear of Coralee," Harper warned. "Otherwise, she'll put you to work."

Sam tried to place the connection. It must've shown on his face because Harper explained, "Coralee is Rigby's grandmother. She's heavily involved in community events and always tries to rope Rigby into doing something for charity."

"The name sounds familiar." Where had Sam heard it before?

"Douglas and Coralee are together," Harper said. She let out a sly giggle as she looked at Scarlett and Rigby. "It makes life interesting."

Sam's eyes widened. "That's right." He looked at Scarlett. "Douglas is your grandfather and Coralee Breeland is Rigby's grandmother." He'd heard Felicia and Jan wagging their tongues about that.

"Yep, it's a tangled web," Rigby quipped as he winked at Scarlett, pulling her close.

"All right, folks. Time's a wasting," Harper said. "Let's get over to the dunking booth."

Sam made a face. "Uh, I think I've changed my mind."

"Too late." Harper grabbed his hand and dragged him through the crowd. The other two followed. Harper stopped beside the booth. Sam let out a sigh. He looked through the plexiglass. Mayor Tate sat on the seat above the water tank.

A young boy around nine or ten years old picked up a softball. "Ready, Dad?"

"Give it your best shot, Keerin," the mayor encouraged.

The crowd cheered. Keerin wound his arm, rocked back on his heels, and launched the ball. It sailed over the booth and out of sight.

"Oh, Keerin. We have some practicing to do," the mayor lamented.

A rather chubby woman stepped up to Keerin and handed him a dollar. "Throw another one, son," she said with a wink.

"Thanks, Mom," Keerin said.

Sam had never met the mayor's wife, but it made sense. The two seemed well suited. A few polite claps sounded as Keerin threw the ball. It hit the plexiglass and fell to the ground. It was obvious that the crowd was only mildly interested in seeing Keerin try to dunk his father.

"Who else wants to try?" asked the teenager running the booth.

A bald man stepped up as Keerin moved to turn away. The man grasped Keerin's shoulders and placed him where he wanted him to be. "Now, that should give you a better vantage point." He handed the teen a dollar before calling out to Mayor Tate. "You shoulda voted with me on that zoning issue last month, Your Honor." He grinned.

Keerin was enjoying this. With a Texas-sized grin, he let the ball loose. It went straight into the ground. People started crowding around, suddenly interested in the action. Ten people lined up behind Keerin, waving their dollars.

"Hey, mayor. Fix that pothole in front of my house."

"Mayor Tate. Our water costs too much."

"Get someone to rake the leaves in the park."

"Have them paint the gazebo while they're at it."

Keerin threw baseball after baseball. After about a dozen tries, he got lucky and hit the target. The ball just bounced off though and His Honor stayed dry.

With a surly wink at Scarlett, Rigby stepped up. "Nice throw, Keerin," he said, and handed his dollar to the teenager.

"Wow, Rocket Breeland," Keerin said in awe. "Are you gonna throw?"

"Sure am, like this." Rigby bent down and picked up Keerin under his arms. He carried him over to the dunking booth and pretended he was going to throw him. Keerin threw the ball from two feet away but still missed. Rigby laughed and swung Keerin's feet so that he kicked the target. The seat swung aside and Mayor Tate fell into the water with a huge splash.

"Got you, Daddy!" Keerin squealed and the crowd roared their approval. Rocket set him down on the ground and extended a hand to the wet mayor.

"Need some help, Your Honor?"

"Thanks, Rocket," the mayor said. He swung a leg over the side and let Rigby pull him out of the water.

The teenager pulled the target back beside the tank. "All right folks, all right. Let me reset the seat, and we'll get our next victim, uh, I mean volunteer." He flashed a huge grin, pleased at his own joke. It took the teen only a moment to swing the target back into place and set up the seat. He picked up a clipboard. "Dr. Wallentine!"

Sam tried to melt into the crowd, but he couldn't hide. Several hands pushed him forward. Finally, he raised his hand.

"All right sir, come on in." The teen set a chair next to the tank. "Do you know how to swim?" he teased.

Sam took off his watch and handed it to Harper, along with his wallet, phone, and sunglasses. He waved and climbed into the seat while the crowd applauded. "Keerin," Sam yelled. "Where did you go?" This earned Sam a few chuckles.

No one stepped up to throw the baseball. "Come on, folks," called the teen. "Support the Women's League. Step right up." Some people in the crowd started to fade away but most of them stayed to see what would happen. "Only a dollar. Come on. Dunk the doc." He paused. "Are you afraid of disrespecting the doc? He's a good sport, and he's looking way too dry."

There was some movement on the edge of the crowd. Rigby stepped forward.

"Hey, no fair," Sam argued. "He's a pro."

Rigby grinned. "And I pay pro rates to support the League." He handed over a fistful of bills. "Don't worry, doc. I won't knock you off." He gave the ball to Harper as he waved to the teenager. "Better bring some more balls."

With a grin, the teen dragged over a basket filled with a dozen baseballs.

Harper took a pitcher's stance. She pointed at Sam. "You're going down, doc."

"Bring your best stuff," he taunted.

Harper's feistiness came out full force as she jutted out her chin, her face a mask of concentration. Her first throw bounced off the backboard and ricocheted into the water. The second whizzed dangerously close to Sam's head. "Oops. Sorry about that," she giggled. He caught number three and tossed it back.

"You throw like a girl!" Sam taunted. The crowd laughed louder.

Harper paused. She squinted and looked hard at the target. After rubbing the ball with her hands, she wound up and threw it. This time she scored a bull's eye. The target swung out of the way with a clang, and Sam fell feet-first into the tub of water. The crowd roared their approval.

Sam climbed over the edge of the tub, dripping water. He held his arms out wide. "I have a big hug for you, babe," he said loudly.

"Get away from me!" Harper ran toward Scarlett and Rocket, but they stepped aside and let Sam grab her from behind. He put his arms around her and pulled her close.

"Just sharing the love," he proclaimed with a laugh. The glow in Harper's eyes made Sam feel warm all over, despite being wet.

The teenager threw them a semi-dry towel. Sam used it to mop the water from his face and hair.

Harper grimaced. "I guess I should've asked you to do the dunking booth earlier, so you would've thought to bring a change of clothes."

"A little water won't kill me," he said bravely then faked a shiver. "Hopefully, I won't get hypothermia."

"No chance of that, doc. I'll keep you warm," Harper patted his cheek, her gaze settling on his lips.

"I'll hold you to that," Sam said.

He dried for a minute or so and hung the towel on a tree branch as the high school principal climbed into the dunking tank.

Harper grabbed Sam's hand. "Come on," she said eagerly. "Let's go ride some rides."

CHAPTER 9

They went through the mirrors and rode the gravity spinner. When Sam and Harper went through the Tunnel of Love, Harper scooted close and managed to get in a long, intimate kiss that sent them both into a tailspin. Sam admitted that the scenario reminded him of a teenager, trying to sneak in a kiss. Harper just laughed and replied with a throaty, "No teenager ever kissed me like that."

The sun settled lower and soon was a gleaming light shining through the pines. "Rigby, come ride the Ferris Wheel," Scarlett said. Her eyes sparkled with hidden meaning as she looked at Harper. "You two should join us."

Sam was surprised and intrigued when Harper blushed. Reaching for her hand and linking her fingers through his, Sam leaned closer. "What's the story with you and Ferris Wheels?"

The color in Harper's cheeks deepened. "It's nothing."

"Come on," he persisted.

She hesitated like she wouldn't tell him, but finally rolled her eyes. "I've always been a sucker for Ferris Wheels. You know, the stolen kiss in the sky from Prince Charming."

A grin tugged at his lips. "I always suspected that beneath your tough, working-woman exterior you were a romantic at heart."

She laughed. "The truth is out."

He pursed his lips. "There's only one problem."

Amusement simmered in her eyes. "Oh, yeah?"

"Too late." He adopted a regretful frown. "We already lived out that fantasy in the Tunnel of Love," he uttered.

Harper blinked, her face reddening again. She gave him an appraising look as she laughed. "You are charming."

The Ferris Wheel was larger than Sam expected. It was a gondola style, allowing the four of them to sit together. Sam was mostly dry by this point, but he still enjoyed the warmth Harper's body offered as she sat close to him. When their gondola was at the top, it paused as the operator let more riders in at the bottom of the wheel. They had a view of the whole town. The streetlights made glowing circles on the ground.

"It's so much quieter up here than it is down there in the crowd," Scarlett observed.

Rigby cocked his head. "Listen. You hear that?"

Everyone strained to hear. "What?" Scarlett asked.

"There's a dog barking way over yonder. You hear it?" A cocky grin slid over his lips as everyone laughed.

Scarlett shoved him. A second later, she pointed. "Look, there's The Magnolia."

"There's your office, Sam," Harper said. "From here it looks so small ... hey, who's that?"

Two figures walked along the side of Clementine Medical Care. They paused at each window and peered in. One of them walked around front and tried the door. Rigby recognized them first. "That's Peter and Judd. I haven't seen them in a dozen years. When did they get back?"

"About a week ago," Harper responded darkly. "They've been up to no good ever since."

"I'm sure they feel like the town's ripe for picking now that everyone's at the fair," Sam observed. No, more accurately, they felt like his office was ripe for the picking. They were probably hoping to find some narcotics. Although for that, the logical choice would be the pharmacy as the clinic only had handfuls of random samples. Then again, these hooligans probably didn't realize that.

Scarlett pulled out her cell phone and dialed 911. "Hello … I'm at the fair on the Ferris Wheel. We spotted prowlers at the doctor's office in Clementine … No, they haven't broken in yet but they're checking it out … looking in all the windows. Yes, we know who they are. They've both served time and have only been back in town for a few days—Judd Barber and Peter Morrison." A second later, Scarlett ended the call. "The dispatcher said she'd send someone to check it out."

"I imagine Chief Alden and the deputies are here at the fair," Rigby said.

Sam's gut tightened. The need to get off the Ferris Wheel and do something to protect his turf was overwhelming. He looked at the tense faces around him and knew they were thinking the same thing. It occurred to Sam that the people around him cared about him and his livelihood. He was making lifelong friends who would share in the ups and downs that life afforded. No, they were more than friends. Sam looked at Harper, his love for her swelling within him. If Sam had anything to say about it, Rigby and Scarlett would one day be his extended family.

With a jerk, the wheel started turning again.

When they got to the bottom, Scarlett waved to the kid running the controls. "Hey, we need to get off."

The kid didn't look up from his phone. He had earbuds in to drown out the grinding motor next to him. The wheel kept going around. When they got to the top, Sam looked for the two potential intruders around his office. He couldn't see them. The wheel dipped them below the treetops, and then up again. The duo was walking back across the front of the office.

Harper and Scarlett yelled in unison when they passed the bottom of the rotation. "Stop this thing and let us off," Harper ordered, but whether the guy heard them or not, he didn't acknowledge, still intent on his phone screen.

Back up they went. Sam kept hoping to see a police car or something, but nothing. Finally, on their next revolution they saw a police car roll to a stop in front of Sam's office.

"About time," Harper muttered.

Two figures darted from the rear of the office property into the alley behind and jogged down the block until they reached the street. They started walking down the sidewalk away from the office and disappeared out of the streetlight glow and into the darkness.

Sam and Harper sat back in their seats. "Where's the closest place to buy a surveillance system?" Sam asked.

"Probably over in Montgomery," Scarlett answered.

They reached the bottom and the operator stopped the Ferris Wheel to let them off. "You really should get off your phone and pay more attention to your job," Harper snapped as she passed the Ferris Wheel operator. The boy's jaw went slack, and he threw up his hands like he had no idea what Harper was talking about.

"Down girl," Scarlett warned as she pulled Harper's arm to move her away from the boy.

"I was just giving him a good lesson in business ethics," Harper protested.

Scarlett hooted. "Yep, with a bit of Harper Boyce tongue lashing mixed in."

A begrudging smile pulled at Harper's lips as she rolled her eyes.

"Scarlett and I are in town for the weekend. It shouldn't be too hard to find a system," Rocket said. "I'll help you install it."

"Rocket, you don't know anything about that sort of stuff," Scarlett chided.

"If a pro football quarterback and a board-certified surgeon can't figure it out, nobody can," Rigby retorted.

"Sounds like a double date," Harper said, her irritation at the operator dissolving in the wake of a large smile.

"Thank you," Sam said, grateful for the help. Watching helplessly while those criminals tried to break into his office was unnerving. A sense of foreboding swept over him. Why did he get the feeling that he'd not seen the last of Judd Barber and Peter Morrison?

CHAPTER 10

"*M*orning," Andi said breezily as she strolled into Harper's office at the restaurant and sat down across from her desk.

"Good morning." Harper closed her laptop. She'd gotten here early to go over the inventory list. One thing led to another, and before long, she was pouring over spreadsheets that detailed earnings from the past month.

Andi motioned. "What's the good word?"

"Profits are up and expenditures are down."

"I would've expected nothing less with you at the helm," Andi said with a trace of admiration. "I heard Rigby and Scarlett were in town this weekend. Are they still here?"

"No, they left to go back home this morning."

"So," Andi began, "how was the fair?"

Harper could tell from the sparkle in Andi's eyes that something was up. "It was good," she said warily.

Andi leaned forward, a smile tugging at her lips. "How was the Tunnel of Love?"

Harper's eyes rounded. "Huh?"

"Sissy Mayfield's little brother was sitting in the car behind you and Sam. He saw the two of you making out."

Heat rose in Harper's cheeks. "We weren't making out," she scoffed.

Andi raised an eyebrow. "Really?"

"Okay," Harper admitted with an embarrassed laugh. "We might've shared a teensy little kiss." She held up her hand, her index finger and thumb an inch apart to gauge the measurement.

"That's not what I heard."

Harper rocked back. "What did you hear?"

A coy smile spread over Andi's lips. "That the doc was giving you a thorough tonsil inspection."

Harper gurgled a cough. A second later, she and Andi were both doubled over in laughter. A few minutes later, Harper mopped her eyes. "Oh, the joy of living in a small town. You can't sneeze without the news spreading like wildfire."

Andi gave Harper a speculative look. "I take it things are going well with the doc?"

"They are, as a matter of fact."

"So … should I be expecting wedding bells in the near future?"

"No," Harper scoffed, tension climbing into her shoulders.

Andi gave her a funny look. "I thought you and Sam were the real deal."

"We are," Harper said quickly. She shifted, not wanting to open this conversation, but she knew Andi would press her until she told all. "Sam wants us to move to the next level." She pushed out a dry laugh. "He's ready for the white picket fence, the passel of kids, and the whole shebang."

"I thought that's what you wanted too."

"I do … eventually."

A furrow dented the center of Andi's brows. "What's the problem then?"

Harper sighed. The morning had started off so well … until Andi started giving her the third degree. She sat back in her seat and folded her arms. "You know my history with men."

Andi spread her hands. "So? Sam's different."

"That's what we thought about Warner, remember?"

"It's not the same, Harper. You can't keep holding onto past hurts. What happened with Warner has nothing to do with Sam."

"Now you sound like Sam," Harper said tartly.

Andi's eyes rounded. "You've had this conversation with Sam?"

Harper nodded.

"I don't understand. A wonderful, intelligent, gorgeous man is crazy about you, and you're holding him at bay? What's the matter with you?"

Harper's spine stiffened. She leveled a glare at Andi. "I know it seems like I've lost my mind, but there's a method to my madness."

Andi folded her arms over her chest. "I'm listening."

"You know how Warner's been coming around lately, desperate to get me back?"

"Yeah," Andi said warily.

"Well, that never happened until after I started turning his butt down." The vehemence of her words left her throat raw. "It's a law of nature. Men want what they can't have, plain and simple."

Andi gave her an incredulous look. "Do you think that if you play hard to get, it's going to make Sam want you more?"

"It's worked so far," Harper retorted. She was taken back when she saw the mixture of pity and compassion in Andi's eyes.

"You're crazy about Sam, aren't you?"

Without warning, tears sprang in Harper's eyes. "Is it that obvious?" she asked hoarsely.

"To me, yes, but maybe not to Sam." Andi's head swung back and forth. "This could backfire on you. A man like Sam won't wait around forever. Think about it. You know he has to have tons of women falling over him."

A stab of jealously went through Harper. She didn't like thinking about Sam with anyone else but her.

"You need to be straight with Sam, tell him how you feel."

Harper's stomach tightened into a small, hard ball.

"You know I'm right," Andi said, squaring her jaw.

"I know what I'm doing," Harper fired back.

Andi didn't skip a beat. "You know what happened to the girl who played with matches, don't you?"

Harper grunted.

Andi enunciated every word like a hammer spiking nails into a tired, old plank of wood. "SHE-GOT-BURNED. Do yourself a favor, Harper. Quit playing stupid games and tell Sam how you feel about him. Trust him. Trust yourself."

A single tear dribbled down Harper's cheek. She wiped it away with an impatient flick. Could she let down her barrier and trust again? More than anything, she didn't want to lose Sam. She felt Andi studying her. "What?" she flung back.

Andi leaned forward, locking eyes with her. "Tell him!"

"I just don't get it, doc. This rash was on my arms. They're better, but now it's on my hands and face."

Sam forced his mind to concentrate on Douglas Foster and his malady. Thanks to Rigby's help, Sam had gotten a security system installed, making him feel more at ease.

"Everything okay?" Douglas asked. "You seem a little distant today."

Sam offered an apologetic smile, clearing away the mental cobwebs from the weekend. "I'm going to get to the bottom of this. Is there anything in particular that seems to make it worse?"

"I dunno. Maybe sweating. When I'm working in the garden it seems like my sweat aggravates it. It burns, probably from the salt."

"How about sunlight?"

"Nope, no effect. Not better or worse. But I feel like I can't hold my eyes open. I'm not sleepy. They just like to close on me all the time. My strength's not nearly what it used to be either. My muscles ache a lot even when I'm not working hard. They're weak and they hurt. I know I'm getting old, but this is ridiculous."

"Douglas, you're not old enough for this yet."

"Thanks doc, but yes I am. When you've got more friends in the church graveyard than in Sunday services, you're getting old."

Sam smiled. "It's time we got some blood tests and figured this out. I'm going to have Jan draw a rheumatoid panel, a cell count, and some antibody studies on your blood. It'll take a couple of days for the tests to come back. In the meantime, I'm going to have you take a prescription-strength antihistamine and a short course of steroids. Let me know how it does. Sound good?"

"How should I know? You're the one who went to medical school."

Sam suppressed the urge to grin. Douglas was a crusty fella. "Right. Then I'd say it sounds good," he said decisively. Sam got up from his rolling stool and walked to the door. He paused. "May I ask you a personal question, in confidence?"

"I've got no secrets. Ask away."

"You know your granddaughter, Harper?"

"Yes, I'd say I know her pretty well." A sly grin slid over his lips. "I've seen she's caught your eye."

"Yes, yes of course you know who she is," Sam stammered. "That's not what I meant to say. Harper and I are dating. The two of us are doing well. I care about her a lot, and I think she cares about me." He thought about their kisses, filled with more passion than Sam would've thought possible. Then, there was the tender look in Harper's eyes that spoke volumes. Still, Sam wanted something more definite, more lasting.

"But?" Douglas inserted.

He pushed out a hard breath. The best way to navigate this thing was to push straight through. "I want to get serious, but Harper's holding back." He looked at Douglas. "Can you think of any reason why?" Sam had Harper's explanation about being hurt before, but he wanted to get another perspective from someone who knew Harper much better than he did.

Douglas folded his arms across his chest. "Let me get this straight. A strong, young Army officer is asking for love advice from a sunburned old sergeant?"

Sam let out a frustrated sigh. "Every time I feel like Harper and I are getting closer, she pulls back. What am I doing wrong?"

Douglas chuckled and looked down. "You ain't doing nothing wrong, son. You just gotta give her time. I guess you haven't dated a lot?"

"Yeah, a fair amount, I guess."

Sam had thought he knew what relationships were until he met Harper. Now, he realized that all the others paled in comparison.

Douglas smiled again. "I guess I was lucky. Polly and I got married right out of high school. We couldn't afford nothing though, so I signed up for the National Guard. They sent me across the state line to Fort Benning for Airborne training, and next thing we knew our unit was called up for Vietnam. It sure was hard telling Polly goodbye when I shipped out." He grew quiet. "I'd been in theatre almost nine months when we got the orders to take Hamburger Hill. The NVA on top were throwing everything they had at us, and we were just trying to find a foothold in the mud. A big Claymore mine, their version of it, came sailing through the air and landed ten feet in front of me. The four guys between me and it died instantly. I lay there full of shrapnel, knowing I was going to die too, and all I could think of was Polly. My buddies were dead all around me. There was more lead and steel raining down every-where, but I couldn't see none of it. All I could see was her face, smiling at me, her hair blowing in the breeze." He stopped talking. Sam waited.

"About three weeks later, I landed on a transport down at Pensacola. When the orderlies carried me off the plane there she was, the most beautiful person I'd ever seen." He grinned. "And about the most pregnant I'd ever seen too. She hadn't told me, because she didn't want me to worry. Eventually I healed up and the Army let me go. We had a great life together." He looked Sam in the eyes. "When you get the kind of love that can survive something like that, you've got something worth going after. Until then all you can do is keep working at it. When it happens, you'll know it."

Sam bowed his head. He'd been privileged to listen to something

... well, something sacred. Douglas and Polly had what every human wanted but few achieved.

"And until then, you'd better treat my granddaughter with all the respect she deserves." He gave Sam a steely look. "I maybe be old, but I'm not dead. If you hurt Harper, I'll hunt you down and make you regret ever meeting her."

"I'd expect nothing less, Sarge."

"Not too long ago, Harper got her heart stomped on by some slick-talking out-of-towner."

"Warner," Sam supplied. He'd only seen Warner once, but his distaste for the man was growing by leaps and bounds, especially considering it was impacting his and Harper's relationship.

"Yep, that's him." Douglas's brows drew together in a sharp v. "If I ever see that weasel, I plan to give him a piece of my mind." He balled his fist.

"Get in line," Sam muttered.

A trickle of amusement mingled with admiration seeped into Douglas's eyes. "It seems the situation's in capable hands. You've got this, doc. Give Harper time. She'll come around."

Sam had hoped that Douglas would give him something more specific. He was giving Harper time, but how much time was he supposed to give her? Speaking of time, Sam realized that he was still on the clock. "Thanks. I'd better get moving. I'd love to talk more but there are people waiting for me. Go ahead and roll up your sleeve. Jan will be here in a couple of minutes." With a farewell nod, Sam stepped out and closed the door behind him.

Felicia was walking up the hall toward her desk. Sam pulled her into the break room. "I've been visiting with Douglas Foster. What happened to Polly?"

Her features pulled down. "Oh, that's a sad story. I was just a little girl. She caught cancer when their second baby was only two or three months old. I never knew her, but I remember my mama telling me how she suffered. It just about broke Douglas into pieces. When people around here talk about what it would be like to have a perfect marriage, they always use Douglas and Polly Foster as their example."

She shook her head. "Poor Douglas. He doted on those babies and raised them up into beautiful young women. I was still in middle school when the older one got married. Then her sister found a guy and got married about a year later. I don't remember what her husband did for work, but he had to go accept some kind of an award over in Montgomery and on the way back a drunk driver killed all four of them. None of them survived. After that, he took in Scarlett like she was his own child."

"Harper went to live with her daddy's sister's family here in town. You've never seen a more devoted father than Douglas was to Scarlett, even though he's her grandpa. It's no surprise he's so crusty. He just wanted to protect her, and now that Rocket Breeland's swept her off to Atlanta to live. I bet he feels that way about Harper too."

"He's definitely crusty," Sam agreed, "but on the inside he's soft and tender. Maybe like a stale, jelly-filled donut."

She wrinkled her nose. "That's a weird analogy, but okay."

"A moldy donut, at that."

Felicia laughed. Jan walked past the door then came back and stuck her head in, her eyes lit with interest. "What did I miss?"

"A juicy gossip session," Sam teased. "Time to get back to work. I've put orders in Douglas's chart for his blood work. Who's next?"

"Mrs. Tate has a big cyst on her back that she wants you to dig out. I have everything set up for you." Jan flashed a devilish grin. "Have fun."

CHAPTER 11

S am came out to the physician's parking area at Daphne Regional Hospital. He put a hand on the anesthesiologist's shoulder. "Thanks again. I enjoyed working with you."

"No problem." A wry grin slipped over his mouth. "I'm not sure Mr. Harrison enjoyed it though. He just kind of laid there, drooling."

Sam grimaced. "He's going to wake up hating me in the morning. I've never had a Nissen fundoplication myself, but I imagine they can't feel too good the day after. Peeling a layer of muscle off the bottom of someone's diaphragm and wrapping it around the top of their stomach has got to be traumatizing."

"Yeah, but you tied it up in such a pretty little bow around his esophagus. I'm afraid he won't like me either. Waking up from ketamine can be pretty unpleasant."

"Then let's put as much distance between us and this place as we can," Sam said with a laugh. "Do you live close by?"

"Kind of. I'm on Lake Alamoosa north of town. It's close enough I can get here in an emergency. You?"

"I've got a small farm a little more than two-thirds of the way to Clementine."

"You mean, being the only doctor in town isn't enough to keep you busy? You have to be a farmer too?"

Sam chuckled. "It keeps me out of trouble. See you next week, Dave."

"Right. See you then." Sam watched Dave climb into his gleaming metallic blue Corvette. He walked down the row of cars to his own and climbed in. He was about to push the start button when he saw a note in his windshield wiper. He got back out and retrieved it. The font was a fancy cursive, printed on a computer.

Hi, doc. You have a fun evening ahead. Meet me at Dogwood Park picnic area at six o'clock. Come prepared for an evening of excitement.

It was signed with a pair of hearts but no name. He brought the paper to his nose. It was adorned with cologne.

A large grin filled his face. Finally, Harper was taking the lead. Had Douglas spoken to her? Good ole Douglas. Sam owed him one. He glanced around. Dave had already left. Where was Dogwood Park? It was fourteen minutes until six. He'd better hurry. With no one around to ask, he started his car and typed Dogwood Park into the GPS. There it was, in the opposite direction out of Daphne from Clementine. The screen showed him that it was eighteen minutes away. He'd better hurry.

He backed out of the parking space and left the lot, almost forgetting to stop for the exit gate arm to go up. It couldn't move fast enough for him. He didn't run any red lights but certainly got through some pinkish ones as he left the town behind. Thirteen miles down the highway there was the brown sign pointing the way toward Dogwood Park. He made a few turns, found the entrance, and followed the guideposts to the picnic area. There were three tables. Only one of them was occupied. It had a white tablecloth, gleaming china and silver, candlesticks, and tall goblets. Harper had pulled out all the stops. Impressive.

Sam got out of his car and walked toward the table. Steaks sizzled on a nearby charcoal grill. Music lilted softly from a small rectangle speaker on the bench. Obscured from view by a large tree in front of the grill, Sam saw her. She had on a yellow sundress with red flowers, which floated gently in the afternoon breeze. Her red high heels were out of place for a picnic but still nice. Harper was so focused on cooking that she hadn't heard him pull up.

Sam walked around the tree. His shoe snapped a twig on the ground, and she spun around with a smile.

Pepper? Why was she cooking for him and Harper?

She held the long grilling fork in her hand and stepped toward him. "Well, hello there, handsome. Surprised?"

Sam blinked. "Yeah. That would be one word for it. How're you doing?" Awkward greeting, but he couldn't think of anything else to say. There were two steaks on the grill. "Uh, there must be some mistake. I got a note on my windshield."

"That's right."

You dummy, his mind shouted. She's not cooking for Harper. *This is for you and Pepper.*

"Other than trying to keep the flies off our food, the mosquitoes off me, and slaving over a hot fire on a sweltering day in South Alabama, I'm doing okay. But that doesn't matter." A large smile ruffled her lips. "You're here now. We can get started."

Pepper's hair and makeup were flawless. Her lipstick was a shade of bright red that complemented her just right. Sam couldn't tell if her eyelashes were real or fake.

Something squeezed Sam's heart, something cold and frightening. He had to get out of here. How about if he turned and sprinted to his car? Could she keep up? Not in those heels. He started backing up.

Her smile faltered. "Where are you going?"

"This isn't a good idea. I'm with Harper."

Pepper trilled out a cheerful laugh. "I know that, silly."

"You do?"

"Sure, I respect that. I just wanted to do something nice for you. You purchased your home from me, after all. And, you've done so much good in Clementine. This is just a small way for me to show my appreciation."

"That's not necessary," he said stiffly. "Harper wouldn't like me being out here with you."

"Oh, she knows."

For a second, Sam thought he'd misheard her. "Huh?"

Pepper nodded. "I had lunch at The Magnolia today. I told Harper I was making you dinner to thank you for buying a house from me."

That didn't sound right. Was Pepper telling the truth? If so, then how could Harper not care that he was having dinner with another woman? His insides tightened.

"You're upset," Pepper purred. "Harper didn't mind us having dinner together, because she knows it's purely platonic."

He made a point of looking at her dress, his eyes settling on her red heels. "Seriously? Do you wear that dress for all your 'platonic' gatherings?"

She giggled. "I had an appointment before I came here and didn't have time to change."

It was an unlikely story, but whatever.

"Sit yourself down, doc," she breathed, clearly flustered. "Let's just enjoy our meal, okay?" She gave him a doe-eyed look. "Please? I've gone to all this trouble."

Sam was trapped. He felt like an opossum in one of those live-catch cages with all the doors shut and kids poking sticks through the wires. How could he get out of this without being rude to Pepper? Then again, Pepper had no right to assume that Sam would be okay with this. Sam was no idiot. Regardless of what Pepper said, he could tell when a woman was into him. Well, at least he thought he could … until Harper. Talk about mixed signals. He'd gotten the note and had been almost giddy, thinking that Harper was taking initiative, only to get here and learn that Harper was perfectly okay with him having dinner with another woman. No, not just another woman, but one who was the favorite subject of the Clementine rumor mill. For the moment, the best course of action was to let the scene play out and watch for an opportunity to escape.

Sam sat down, a dark mood settling over him.

Pepper turned back to the grill and stuck the fork into the steaks. "I hope you like yours medium rare," she said. "They're not bleeding but still pink and juicy in the middle."

"I'm not a connoisseur of steak, I'm afraid," he said dourly, thinking of Harper's gourmet grilled cheese sandwiches. What he would give to have one of them right now. "All throughout my career before I came to Alabama, every steak I ever had was served the Army way: cooked until it and everything in it was dead."

"You just let me handle everything then, darling," she cooed. "I'll teach you everything I know."

"Sounds good. I've got three minutes," he said dryly.

Pepper cocked her head like she was confused by his comment, but Sam could tell that she didn't realize he'd just given her a backhanded insult. Sam drew in a breath. Pepper had gone to a lot of trouble to prepare this meal, and Sam was throwing around cloaked insults. He'd politely eat it and be on his way. Notwithstanding the vicious gossip, Pepper seemed like a decent person. She was a little flashy and gaudy for Sam's taste. He thought of Harper's natural glow, how she was beautiful even with little or no makeup. A longing for Harper swept over Sam. As soon as this meal was over, he planned to visit Harper, question why she was okay with him having dinner with Pepper. More than anything, Sam needed reassurance that Harper felt the same way about him as he did her.

His thoughts moved back to Pepper. He felt for her. She had to be lonely, raising her kids alone. Someplace out there, there was a man for Pepper. It just wasn't him.

"Here you go." Pepper served up the steaks on the plates at the table. She'd cooked green beans with bacon, rolls, and potato salad. There was a pecan pie for dessert. "I'm afraid I don't do pie crusts very well, but I've had this brand before, and it's really good."

Sam glanced around the table, thinking of Harper's mouthwatering sweet potato pie, made from scratch. There were a few things Sam could have taught Pepper, but he held his tongue. No sense being a jerk. Steaks probably should be cooked hot enough and long enough to kill any parasites. Potato salad will grow staphylococcal food poisoning if it sits out in the hot Alabama sun for more than thirty minutes. Gnats will land in chilled apple juice and drown there. He smiled to himself thinking how Harper would accuse him of being a prudish doctor if she could hear his thoughts.

The dinner conversation revolved mostly around Sam's new house that Pepper helped him buy. "I sure would've thought you'd be a country club kind of man, but if you're happy on the farm for the time being then I'm happy, and that's all that matters," she said.

When they'd finished eating, Sam stood. "Thanks so much." He was beyond ready for this awkward dinner to end.

"Do you mind helping me clean up?"

"Sure.

Sam took the pitcher of water and poured it over the coals in the grill. "Let me get that," he said and picked up the bowl of potato salad.

"Everything goes in these." Pepper pulled out some grocery store reusable bags.

"Okay. Got the plates." He set things in the bags with the goblets on top.

Pepper picked up the tablecloth and shook the crumbs off it. "Here, I'll get the other end," Sam said, grabbing the other two corners. He held them up, waiting for her to bring her side to his. Instead, she stepped into him and grabbed his neck. Before he could react, she kissed him full on the mouth.

Shock rattled through him as he jerked back. He looked down, realizing he was still holding his end of the tablecloth, the other side dragging the ground. He glared at Pepper. "What was that for?"

"A little token for you to remember the evening," she said with a seductive grin.

Anger splashed through his veins. "You said this was purely platonic."

"I guess that depends on your definition of platonic." Her eyes sizzled with mischief.

Suddenly the truth came to him in a sickening realization. "You never talked to Harper today." He saw the answer in Pepper's eyes.

Disgust wrangled his gut. "Let me be crystal clear. I have no interest in you whatsoever." Pepper's face fell as he barreled on. "The only woman I'm interested in is Harper Boyce." He clenched his jaw. "You got that?"

Pepper's eyes hardened to flint as she lifted her chin. "Got it," she barked.

He shook his head, a deep weariness overtaking him as he turned and stalked to his car. Talk about a sucker! He was at the top of the list. As he started the engine only one question kept running through his mind.

How in the heck was he going to explain this to Harper?

CHAPTER 12

*T*he next morning dawned bright and beautiful. It was one of those mornings Alabama was famous for, gracing the air with a moist, warm breeze that carried scents of jasmine, honeysuckle and gardenia. Sam put the top down on the Lexus, enjoying the warm sun on his face.

As it turned out, he hadn't been able to talk to Harper the night before because she'd worked late. Even after having time to mull it over, he still hadn't figured out how he was going to explain last night's debacle to Harper, but he knew he had to say something. He had little doubt that Pepper would tell everyone her version of the story.

Arriving at the office ten minutes before opening time, he walked in the front door to find a lobby filled with waiting patients. A few were sneezing and blowing into tissues. Apparently, the honeysuckle and gardenia weren't as enjoyable for everyone as they were for him. There was Maryanne Wheatley who came in at least once a week with some new ailment she'd read about online and knew she must have it. Walter Pinford was back for his quarterly diabetes check so Sam could scold him for not taking his pills or watching his diet. Afterward, Walter would go back to his apple pie and fried chicken.

Felicia stood up at the front desk as he came in and reached through the check-out window to unlock the door from the lobby, so he could enter. "Good morning, Dr. Wallentine. How's your day so far?"

Felicia rarely called him Dr. Wallentine. Was that an edge he detected in her voice? "Morning, Felicia. Just the usual. It's nice weather today."

She grunted in response.

Irritation crawled up Sam's neck as he wondered what was eating at Felicia. Normally, she was the picture of Southern grace. He searched her face. "Is everything okay?"

"You tell me." She arched an eyebrow.

Felicia closed the door and followed him to the back office. Jan was getting ready to call the first patient into a room. "How was your picnic?" Felicia asked.

He stopped in his tracks, his heart picking up its beat. "My what?"

"Have you ever heard of *The Clementine Connection*?" Jan asked.

"How could you do it?" Felicia blurted in a hurt tone that was battered with frustration.

"Do what?" His thoughts tumbled over and over themselves. Felicia had heard about the picnic. Did that mean Harper had? Sam tried calling Harper this morning, but it went to voicemail. He sent her a text as well, but she hadn't responded. Sam hadn't thought twice about it, figuring it was still early in the morning. He assumed Harper would call when she had a minute. Now, however, he wondered if Harper's silence pointed to something more ominous.

Sam reached for the hook on the back of his office door and grabbed his stethoscope. Felicia, not old enough to be his mother but stern enough to be an older sister, put a hand on his chest and pushed him into the office. Jan followed. She sat down in Sam's desk chair and signed onto his computer.

Felicia sighed heavily. "Look doc, Clementine is a small town. Somebody is watching everything you do." She motioned with her eyes. "Show him, Jan."

Jan turned the screen around. There was a page that looked like a newspaper with a color picture of Pepper in her yellow, flowery picnic dress, holding up a pecan pie. The headline read *Afternoon Dalliance Turns Romantic.*

Jan clicked on an arrow beneath the picture. A cheesy rendition of *Strolling Through the Park One Day* started playing on the computer's speakers. "Your nine-twenty a.m. patient writes this blog anytime there's juicy gossip to report. And today, you're it," Jan said sourly.

As Sam scanned the page his heart dropped. "Dr. Sam Wallentine seems to have found a new romance," the story began. "We have it from a reliable source that on yesterday afternoon he went straight from the operating room to operating at Dogwood Park near Daphne. The patient was our own Pepper McClain who was deliciously dressed for the occasion in the sundress shown above. Dr. Sam, of course, looked exceedingly handsome in his hospital scrubs." The article spelled out the menu Pepper had prepared. "The evening concluded with a steamy kiss. Looks like Miss Harper Boyce is going to be up against a challenger for the surgeon's heart."

Acid washed up the back of Sam's throat. He wanted to punch something! He'd been ambushed. Now the entire town would connect him with Pepper. That probably included Harper, if she ever read this piece of trash.

Felicia guessed his thoughts. "I imagine Harper has already seen this, or if she hasn't someone's gonna tell her as soon as she gets to the restaurant."

He looked at the sullen faces of his staff members, feeling the desperation of a condemned man being led to the hangman's noose. "This is not what it looks like."

The women just looked at him with stony expressions.

He ran both hands through his hair. "As I was leaving the hospital last night, there was a note on my windshield. I thought it was from Harper. When I got to the park, Pepper was there."

"So, you had dinner with her and kissed her?" Felicia asked incredulously.

"I didn't kiss Pepper, she kissed me." This was bad. Really bad. He looked pleadingly at the women who worked with him on a daily basis. With a sinking heart, he realized if they didn't believe he was innocent, he didn't have a prayer of anyone else believing him. "Harper means everything to me," he said, his voice quivering with intensity.

"So, it was a setup," Jan said, relief sounding in her voice.

"You're darn right," Sam hurled through clenched teeth. He strode over to the window and glanced up the street. There was no movement at The Magnolia and the lights weren't on. The practical side of his brain took control. "Jan, room my first few patients. Felicia, no same-day appointments this morning. I'm going to see everyone who's scheduled, and then take a long lunch." He was frantic but not panicking. Somehow, he managed to maintain his composure.

Sam went in to see his first patient. Normally, he used diplomacy when talking to his patients, even when Sam knew they had no intention of following his well-intended advice. This time, however, he didn't bother sugar-coating the situation as he spelled out in no uncertain terms exactly what the diabetes would do to Mr. Pinford if he continued down his course of self-destruction. Ten minutes later, Mr. Pinford exited the room. His face was flushed, and he seemed in a hurry. Felicia smiled at him as he passed the check-out window. "Would you like to make a follow-up appointment, Walter?" she asked.

"Not right now, thanks. I'll call you." He walked through the lobby and left.

Sam's anger had cooled to a slow simmer. "Who's my next patient?"

"Maryanne Wheatley," Felicia announced. Her eyes were large like she wondered how Sam would react.

It was Maryanne's slanderous blog that was the cause of the turmoil. The heat turned up, causing the kettle to boil.

Sam picked up the chart off the door. He smoothed his hair back and turned the doorknob. "Good morning, Mrs. Wheatley," he said briskly as he walked in. When he sat down on his stool, movement caught his eye in the light coming under the door. Two pairs of shadows blocked the narrow slit from the hallway lights. It meant Jan and Felicia were up against the door listening. Good. The more witnesses the better.

"Good morning, doctor," Maryanne said pleasantly. "I've been doing some research on the internet, and I found this." She handed Sam a sheaf of papers stapled together. "I'd like you to read it and decide how to treat me."

He took the papers in his hand, his mind snapping over the headline:

Any Exposure to Asbestos Can Contribute to Mesothelioma

Sam sighed. "Mrs. Wheatley, have you ever worked directly with asbestos?"

"No," she said. "But I'm sure some of the older buildings around here have it on their pipes."

"Has anyone disturbed the alleged asbestos on any of these pipes? Has any asbestos dust been released into the air?"

"I—I'm not sure."

"Asbestos dust won't be stirred up just because it wants to be. You can have a building full of it and as long as no one disturbs it, there's no danger whatsoever. Do you smoke?"

"I tried it when I was a teenager. It made me sick, so I didn't start seriously until after my first marriage. I wanted to quit when I got pregnant but couldn't manage to stop until after my third baby was born." She lifted her chin. "Haven't picked one up since, and that was twenty-seven years ago."

"Virtually everyone who came down with mesothelioma, whether the mesothelioma was linked to asbestos or not, was a smoker. You can swim in asbestos, and you won't get cancer from it unless you're a smoker."

"Really?"

"Okay, that's probably an exaggeration. I wouldn't recommend swimming in the stuff, but I'm sure you're safe."

She frowned. "That's all good and well, but how are you going to treat me?"

His words flew out like razor-tip darts. "With all the professionalism I can muster, Mrs. Wheatley, which is a lot more than I can say for our local journalist community."

Her face turned crimson. "Why Dr. Wallentine, who are you referring to?" She sounded out of breath. "I'm the only journalist around here."

His eyes narrowed. "You said it." He paused to let it sink in.

"Are you referring to *The Clementine Connection?*" She began fanning her face with her hand.

"Exactly. That gossip rag is dangerous and harmful."

A shocked look crossed Maryanne's face. "I have no idea what you mean," she stammered.

"Mrs. Wheatley, we can't have a good doctor-patient relationship if you choose to lie to me."

Maryanne's expression changed from disbelief to anger. She clutched her neck. "Dr. Wallentine, you don't wanna make an enemy out of me. I can make or break a person's reputation in this town faster than you can blink." She straightened her shoulders. "I wield the power of the written word."

The indignation burning through Sam's veins made him feel like he'd combust. "Be careful what you write, Maryanne. I have connections who can come down here and haul you, and everyone who works with you, before a judge so fast you won't know what hit you. If anyone outside Alabama has read your work, say a certain football player in Atlanta, then your libel becomes a federal crime. I'll make sure you never write or speak or even use a telephone again unless it's attached to the wall of the women's penitentiary."

The color drained from Maryanne's face. Sam knew that no one here had ever seen this side of him before. "I think I'm covered under the First Amendment," Maryanne stuttered.

"That rule lets you say what you want, even if it's not true, but it doesn't protect you from the consequences if you harm someone."

"I haven't harmed anyone." She scooted back on the table, looked off to the side, then folded her arms in a defiant pose.

Sam's voice went into a cool and collected checkmate mode.

"Actually, my business is based on my reputation. I have to protect it. If you cost me clients then that meets the definition of harm."

"Are you saying that having my source link you to Pepper has harmed your reputation? I hardly think so, Dr. Wallentine. She's a lovely girl. Any man would be lucky to be mentioned in the same article with her."

Sam wanted to say that Pepper's first two husbands might argue with that sentiment, but no sense in adding more fuel to feed Maryanne's gossip. "Your insinuation that Pepper and I are romantically involved is completely false."

"You did have dinner with her."

"As friends," he said firmly. "Pepper said the dinner was her way of thanking me for purchasing a home through her agency."

"Likely story," she harrumphed.

He leaned forward. "Who's your source?" He already knew who the culprit was—Pepper herself! Sam just wanted to hear Maryanne say it.

Maryanne started blinking rapidly. "My sources always remain confidential. If I revealed their identities, I'd lose them as sources."

Sam was growing tired of this nonsense. "Good grief," he muttered. "You make it sound like these are world secrets."

She gave him a haughty glare. "For a lot of people here, Clementine is their world, and I'm the daily news. A lot of them never read other news online. The TV news is just full of gloom and murder, so they don't bother watching it. All they know comes from me."

"In that case, my best advice to you is to verify your sources. Publishing lies can get you in a lot of trouble. Likewise, you need to verify your health information sources. That article you brought me is full of half-truths that will also hurt you. It's garbage."

Maryanne put her hand to her bosom. "What?" Her voice rose an octave. "Garbage? I've been taking information from this website for years."

"That doesn't make it true. If you were to repeat it in your column and somebody were to be injured because they acted on it, you'd be responsible for whatever happened to them." Sam pushed out a heavy breath.

It was obvious that neither of them was getting anywhere in their debate. "You don't have mesothelioma. You have no symptoms of it and no risk factors. Now please, I don't mind seeing you if there's really something wrong, but if you keep making appointments for things you don't have, it takes away time from people who truly are sick and need to be seen. Thanks for coming in." He walked out of the room and handed the chart to Jan with a 'get rid of her' look.

Sam walked to his desk and sat down. He'd managed to keep his rage from boiling over while he talked to Maryanne Wheatley, which was a miracle considering how much trouble the busybody had caused him. How was Harper going to take this? Not well. She was already distrustful of men. Now, Sam would have a black mark against him.

Sam went back to work. He froze two warts off Oscar Mortensen's hand. That didn't go well, but it never does when one is applying liquid nitrogen to a five-year-old. Not that adults were much better. Sam refilled Justin Taylor's blood pressure medicine, told Sallie Bridges that she didn't need antibiotics for a sinus infection, cleared Dave Bahr for his trip to the Himalayas, and spent twenty minutes trying to convince Terry van Mann that it was unhealthy for her to keep taking narcotics for her back when she hadn't tried any safer alternatives.

Sam moved through the remaining list of patients robotically until mercifully, the morning ended.

The lobby was empty, and it was time for lunch. "Going over to The Magnolia for a bite, Doc?" Jan asked.

Sam felt a huge weight descend on his shoulders. "I don't know if I can."

Felicia wheeled her chair back from the reception desk. "You better." She wagged a finger, her dark eyes sparking. "Don't leave Harper over there feeling betrayed. You've gotta make this right. Now, drag yourself over there, mister. Crawl if you have to. Show Harper that Maryanne Wheatley's article is all fluff with no substance. Otherwise, you'll lose the chance to set this situation upright on its feet."

"I'm probably the last person Harper wants to see right now," he said glumly.

"That's exactly why you need to get over there. If you don't, Harper will ruminate on this and blow it into something it isn't. You've got to set things straight, even though it's not your fault." She stopped, tipping her head. "You never did explain why you didn't just hightail it out of that park when you realized Pepper was the one cooking you dinner."

He rubbed his neck. "I was an idiot. Pepper said she wanted to thank me for buying a house from her."

"You know, Sam, for all your big-brain medical knowledge, you're pretty dense when it comes to matters of the opposite sex."

"Yeah, I'm learning that the hard way," he said morosely.

She sighed. "All right then, go on over there and explain it to Harper. Beg if you have to."

"Harper's a sensible person, not the kind to make a mountain out of a molehill. Surely, she'll see this for what it is—a setup."

"Uh, don't be so sure. Harper's a woman. Making mountains out of molehills is what we do."

Jan walked up. "Felicia's absolutely right." She propped a hand on her hip. "Unless you go tell Harper what really happened, she's gonna be finished with you. Then, Pepper will have no reason not to shift things into high gear. If you're fine with Pepper then do nothing, but if Harper's the one you're really after, tuck your tail between your legs, and go throw yourself on her mercy. Just don't wait to do it."

Sam was caught in a web, the strands getting tighter by the minute. "The whole town will be watching. Maybe I should talk to Harper in private."

"The whole town reads *The Clementine Connection*. If you got humiliated in public, you should fight it in public." Jan handed him his sunglasses. "I grabbed these off your desk. It's pretty bright outside. You'll need them." When he hesitated, Jan pointed her eyes toward the door. "Whatcha waiting for, Doc Hollywood? Get going."

Sam walked down the front steps to the sidewalk, fully aware of the two faces watching him from his office window. Three doors down, he saw another face on a For Sale sign in front of what had been an accountant's office. Realtor Pepper McClain beamed a smile at all who passed. Scowling, Sam looked away.

Andi was decidedly cool when she greeted Sam at the hostess stand. "Doctor Wallentine. One for lunch?"

He cleared his throat. "Actually, I'd like to speak to Harper."

Hesitation crept into Andi's eyes.

"Would you go tell her I need to talk to her?"

Andi's hand went to her hip, her scathing eyes flickering over him. "Fine," she harrumphed as she went to the back and returned a minute later. "Harper's busy," she retorted smugly. "I can show you to a table if you want lunch."

"I do."

"Follow me." She picked up a menu and led him to a table in the back left corner of the room, away from the kitchen and Harper. Not saying another word, Andi set his menu on the table and walked away with a stiff, unyielding carriage.

Geez. Tough crowd. By now, Sam figured that the majority of Harper's employees had read the blog; discussed it, dissected it, digested it, and spit it out. No doubt they wished they could spit Sam out with it. He glanced around the dining room. It wasn't full, but half the people there seemed to be glaring at him with disapproval.

He buried his face in the menu. He'd never had a grilled tuna salad sandwich. It sounded pretty good. His appetite for food wasn't there, but he couldn't take up a table unless he was buying.

Marie bustled up to the table and plopped down a glass of water.

"Hello," he said tentatively, wondering if Marie would treat him like dirt too.

"Hi, doc," Marie quipped before scuttling away like she didn't want to be seen spending a minute longer than necessary with the enemy.

With a frustrated sigh, Sam turned his attention back to the menu. A couple seconds later, someone bumped his table.

He looked up assuming Marie had returned but Harper was there instead. Scooting back his chair, he moved to stand.

"Don't bother," she said coolly as she sat down across from him.

Sam tried to respond, but his voice didn't work right away. He cleared his throat. "I take it this is about Maryanne Wheatley's blog." No sense beating around the bush.

Harper's face was pale as alabaster, her lips set in rigid lines as she clasped her hands together. Sam saw the hurt in her eyes, but more than that, Harper was furious.

"How could you?" Her voice was a hoarse whisper. "I trusted you."

"That's not exactly true."

She flinched. "What do you mean?"

It probably wasn't the smartest thing to say right now, but Sam was tired of dancing around the topic. "If you really trusted me, we'd be planning our future instead of sitting here having this conversation."

She chortled out a hard laugh. "Says the man who got caught with his hand in the cookie jar." Her eyes narrowed to hard slits. "Or his lips soldered to Pepper McClain's."

"I didn't kiss Pepper," he huffed in exasperation. "She kissed me."

His comment was a waving red flag that enraged the bull. Harper's face turned redder than a sunburn as she drew herself up. "So, you're admitting it. You had a picnic with Pepper, and the two of you kissed." Hurt washed over her features.

"She tricked me, Harper. I thought I was meeting you."

She gave him an astonished look. "That doesn't make a lick of sense. Why would you think that?"

Across the room, waiting in the shadow of the kitchen entrance, Sam saw several of Harper's employees watching closely. They were taking note of his every move, ready to spring to Harper's aid at any moment. Someone should've told them that Harper was no dainty princess. She didn't need anyone's help.

Harper looked him in the eye. "Did you even think about me, or were you just running on testosterone?"

His throat was parched. He reached for his glass and gulped a quick drink. Harper was going for the jugular vein.

"I came out of the hospital and there was a note stuck in my windshield wiper. It said for me to go to Dogwood Park." He met her glare full on, hoping she'd believe the sincerity of his next statement. "I'd go anywhere you asked." He paused, hoping to see a softening of her features, something that would let him know he was getting through to her. Seeing nothing but impenetrable anger, he continued. "I found Dogwood Park and went in. Pepper was standing behind some tree branches at first, I thought she was you. All I could see of her was from the waist down. By the time I realized she was actually Pepper and not you, it was too late."

She cocked an eyebrow, her voice going razor sharp. "Too late? What do you mean?"

"Pepper knew I was there. She already had everything cooked. The dinner was all laid out on the table. Pepper assured me that the dinner was platonic, a simple gesture to thank me for using her as a realtor." Harper remained silent so he continued. "I told Pepper that you wouldn't like me having dinner with another woman."

Harper cackled out a laugh harder than cement. "That was kind of you to remember my feelings."

He rushed on. "Pepper told me that she'd stopped by The Magnolia yesterday during lunch. She said she told you that she was making me dinner and that you were perfectly okay with it."

Harper's jaw dropped. For a second, she was speechless. Slowly, she began shaking her head back and forth. "No!"

"No, what?"

"You're not turning this thing around to make you out to be the victim."

"I am the victim," he fired back, his voice rising.

The creases in her forehead deepened. "You're a big boy. You had to know what Pepper was up to."

"Actually, I didn't. I spent the first part of the dinner trying to wrap my head around the fact that you didn't care if I had dinner with another woman."

Her eyes took on a wild look. "This is absurd. Of course, I care!"

"Well, you don't have a great way of showing it. Every time I've tried to broach the topic of the future, you push back."

She grunted in disgust. "I see what's happening here."

"It's about time," he muttered. "I was set up."

She charged on. "This is some twisted game to get back at me because I wasn't ready to jump full force into marriage the minute you snapped your fingers."

His brow furrowed. "What? I would never do that." He gave her a withering look. "If you really believe that, then you don't know me at all."

Fire raged in her eyes. "Evidently, I don't." Her voice caught. "All this time, you've been trying to convince me that you're not like Warner."

"I'm not."

"No, you're worse than Warner," she spat. "At least Warner took responsibility for his actions when he started fooling around with Pepper. You want to play the victim!"

Sam felt the blood drain from his face. "Warner had a thing with Pepper?" The full scope of the situation hit Sam forcefully, knocking the wind out of him. "Wow, I had no idea." No wonder Harper was going berserk. Compassion welled inside him as he looked across the table at the woman he loved. She was right in front of him, and yet, there was a mile-high wall of misunderstanding between them. He reached for her arm. "I'm sorry," he began. "You have to believe me. There's nothing going on between me and Pepper."

"Don't," she warned, jerking her arm out of his grasp. She stood.

"Harper, please, sit back down, so we can discuss this."

"I'm done talking," she seethed.

He rose to his feet. Desperation seeped into him as he searched her face. "You've got to know how I feel about you."

She jutted out her chin with an iron determination. "The only thing I know right now is that we're through." She turned on her heel and tromped away.

It took all the strength Harper could summon to hold back the avalanche of tears until she got to her office. She slumped down behind her desk, letting the hot tears spill. A second later, there was a single knock at the door before Andi stepped in, closing the door behind her.

Agony sliced ribbons through Harper's stomach. "You were right. I played with matches, and I got burned."

Anger flashed over Andi's features. "No, you were right about Sam. He's a scoundrel." She slumped down in a chair.

"Sam claims that Pepper lured him there and set him up." An image of Sam flashed through Harper's mind. He seemed so sincere. Harper wouldn't put anything past Pepper. She probably had lured Sam to the picnic. Still, that didn't excuse Sam for sticking around.

Andi barked out a laugh. "Likely story."

"That's what I said," Harper said feeling vindicated that Andi was reacting the same way she had. Hurt bulldozed over Harper, making her feel like her heart would crumble in on itself. "I thought Sam was different." She took in a quick breath to stifle a sob. "I took your words to heart. I was gonna move things forward with Sam." She hugged her arms. "Now this." She'd allowed herself to dream of a life with Sam, imagining them having tall and muscular sons with quick-silver smiles and intelligent green eyes like their father. Heck, if the truth be known, Harper had even envisioned a dog and white picket fence.

"I'm so sorry."

Tears streamed down Harper's cheeks. "I love him … loved him," she corrected, balling her fist and bringing it to her chest.

Fury burned in Andi's eyes. "I have a good mind to march back out there and beat the crap out of him."

A short laugh escaped Harper's throat. "You know, I believe you would." Her head was starting to pound. Harper wanted to crawl into a ball and bawl, but there was no time for that. She was a resilient businesswoman who'd weathered plenty of storms in the past. This thing with Sam Wallentine hurt like the dickens, but she refused to let it break her. Sniffling, she staunchly wiped at her tears. "I guess the fairy tale is over, huh?" A sad, wistful smile touched her lips. "Maybe there really is no such thing as happily ever after."

Not having a response, Andi just shook her head and looked away.

A heavy gloom settled between them. Harper just sat there, staring off into space. How much time passed, she didn't know. She sat until her limbs grew stiff. Finally, she stood, her voice dull. "Time to get back to work."

CHAPTER 13

*I*t was a week and a half before Sam saw Harper again. Not wanting to have to deal with the coldness of her employees, Sam had stopped going to The Magnolia for lunch. It was easier to just make a sandwich and bring it with him to the office. Every time Sam so much as looked in the direction of The Magnolia, a pang went through him. He still couldn't believe Harper was so bull-headed about this. Sure, it was foolish to have a picnic with Pepper, but Harper had to know how conniving Pepper was. He grunted. That was the problem—Harper knew Pepper had lured him to the park. She attributed Sam's sticking around to eat as a major weakness or character flaw. It didn't help that Pepper had stolen Warner away from Harper.

He blew out a heavy breath, wishing there was some way he could get through to Harper. It had taken a nearly superhuman effort to stay away from her. The only reason he'd done so was because he hoped that given time to cool off, Harper would view the situation differently. Thankfully, Sam hadn't seen hide nor hair of Pepper since the picnic. That was fine with him. In fact, he hoped to never see the woman again, which wasn't realistic in a small town. But from now on, Sam planned to keep his distance as much as humanly possible.

The time away from Harper was brutal. She'd constantly been on Sam's mind.

Nothing was the same. Work wasn't as fulfilling as it used to be. It was harder to get out of the house and take care of his little farm. His heart wasn't in it anymore. Everything was a hollow shell.

Felicia greeted him when he walked into the office. "A little behind schedule this morning, doc?"

"I had to stop and help with a car wreck on the way here."

Felicia's face fell. "Oh, no, was everybody okay?"

Sam shook his head. "There was only one man involved, but he lost a lot of blood. I'm not sure if he'll make it."

The horror on Felicia's face reflected Sam's own feelings. The wreck occurred a mere mile from his house. A car had spun out of control, hitting a tree. The driver was a man in his young twenties. Sam hadn't been able to tell exactly where the man's injuries were because he'd not wanted to move him. Sam only knew it was around the man's lower spine. He'd done all he could to help until the EMS crew arrived. The incident reminded Sam how fragile life is, leaving a pit in his stomach. He thought of his friends and co-workers in Afghanistan, a cold shiver moving down his spine.

Everything in him wanted to race to Harper's side and pull her into a tight embrace. Harper had lived here in the shelter of Clementine. Had she witnessed the things Sam had, no doubt, she would be less determined to hold a grudge over a misunderstanding. Well, it was more than a mere misunderstanding, Sam admitted. Harper had a right to be upset. She wondered if she could trust Sam. He got that, but how long was Harper going to make him wait for her forgiveness? She'd said the two of them were through, but Sam wasn't willing to accept that. He planned to fight for their relationship. He just didn't know how to go about it yet.

"Are you okay, Sam?" Felicia looked at him with concern.

He forced a smile. "Yeah, it's just hard to see something like that."

She nodded in understanding.

He went into professional mode. "I'll get going, so I can catch up here." He went immediately to the first patient room. Allison Decker was in for a big mole on her cheek that was starting to cave in at the center. "That's a squamous cell cancer," Sam said. "I'd like to take it off right now if you have time."

Tears rose in Mrs. Decker's eyes. "I—I have cancer?" she stammered, clutching her neck.

"The mole is cancerous. I need to remove it."

She nodded. "Dr. Wallentine, if you say it's cancer, I'll make time. Just get it off me."

Sam stepped out of the room. "Jan, set me up with an excision tray for Mrs. Decker." He went into room two. Frank Hollingsworth was there to go over his lab reports. "We'll start you on monthly testosterone injections. In three months, we'll check your blood level again." He went back to room one and injected lidocaine beneath Mrs. Decker's skin cancer. "Let's give this five minutes to get you numb, and then get rid of that monster. You just lie here and relax." He patted her on the shoulder and went to room three. As he passed Jan in the hall, he ordered, "1 ml of testosterone IM for Mr. H, please." In room three he found Jason Hartford in a gown for his football physical. "Do you have some papers for me, Jason?"

"Yes, sir. Here they are."

Sam took the papers. He read through the history section. "That's a really boring medical history, kiddo," he said with a wink. "Isn't there anything more interesting than this?"

"Nope," Jason responded proudly.

They went quickly through the sports clearance exam. Sam put on a glove with a snap. "Anytime your doctor puts on gloves, something bad's about to happen," he said with a grin. "Stand up here, turn your head away from me and cough." He finished up, signed the papers, and went back to room one. Ten minutes later he was snipping his stitches and helping Mrs. Decker sit upright. "How do you feel? Any dizziness or nausea?"

"No. I'm just glad that thing's gone. Thank you. I appreciate it." Her lower lip quivered. "When do we have to start chemotherapy?"

Sam's eyes widened, compassion welling inside him. It was good to be able to deliver some good news, for once. "You won't need chemo for this cancer. Simply cutting it out has an excellent cure rate. I'd like for you to come back in about a month for a good, thorough skin exam though."

She sighed in relief. "Oh, you can count on that."

Sam moved on. His next patient was Stuart Peterson. He'd just turned fifty and was in to get set up for his colonoscopy. Sam gave the usual spiel and handed him two small bottles. "Drink the first one the morning before the procedure along with two quarts of water. Nothing except clear liquids to drink that day. Drink the second bottle with another two quarts instead of supper. Go ahead and take your blood pressure medicine on the morning of the procedure, and I'll see you at the hospital in Daphne at six the next morning."

"Gee, that sounds like a lot of fun," he said dryly. "Thanks a bunch."

"My pleasure," Sam said with a smile.

His next patient was Douglas Foster. He wasn't wearing a smile today. Then again, he never did. "How's the rash, Sarge?"

Douglas grunted. "Worse than ever. Why do you think it won't go away?"

Sam pulled up the lab report on his laptop. "Let me refresh my memory. Your blood tests came back stone cold normal. There's nothing here that looks like rheumatic disease, Sjogren's syndrome, thyroid issues... No, nothing real helpful there. Did the prednisone help?"

He shrugged. "Maybe for a few days. Now it's not just my joints. My bones ache and my muscles are killing me. Sometimes in the mornings I can hardly open my eyes. They're just so weak. And this rash is crazy." He pulled up his sleeves. Broad reddish-purple patches covered his arms. There was a rough red rash on his cheeks.

"Does that itch or hurt?" Sam asked.

"A little, but the main thing is the aching all over. I feel like I'm coming off a three-day drunk, but it's been going on for months."

Sam sat back to run through his differential diagnosis. The problem was, there weren't a whole lot of things that went along with the whole constellation of symptoms. Psoriatic arthritis wasn't out of the question but the rash wasn't right. It wasn't likely scleroderma. He was too old for myasthenia gravis. "Did you ever have strep throat when you were little?"

"Well sure. Who didn't?"

"Mm hmm." Sam thought a little longer. Rash. Muscle pain. Joint pain. Temporary improvement with steroids. Suddenly the light went on. He opened his mouth to speak but was interrupted by a knock on the door. "Come on in," he said automatically.

Jan opened the door. She looked over her shoulder to the hall. "Here you go. Have a seat."

Harper walked in. Sam's breath caught in his throat. Harper had that natural beauty that made blue jeans look great, but also was just right for Sunday best. It didn't matter what Harper wore. She was just naturally beautiful. His heart started racing, and it was all he could do to keep his expression placid.

"Hello, Sam," she said simply in a tone so neutral that it was impossible to gauge her anger towards him.

When he regained his composure, he managed to squeak, "Hi, Harper. We were just talking, and I was about to say—" He looked at Douglas. "What was I about to say?" *Geez.* How was he supposed to think straight with Harper here? He wanted to pull her into his arms and kiss her until neither of them could breathe. Then, he wanted to tell Harper about the wreck, explaining that their relationship and time together was precious, because no one was guaranteed a tomorrow.

"You were about to tell me what I've got," Douglas grumbled.

"Right, right. Looks like you have a condition called dermato-myositis. *Derm* means skin, *myo* means muscles, and *itis* means inflammation. It can be a disease all by itself, but sometimes it's more of a symptom of another disease like lupus. Have you ever heard your parents or your brothers and sisters say they had anything like you're experiencing?"

"No, never did."

"Grandpa, what about Aunt Mabel?" Harper pitched in. The worry in her expression made Sam want to help soothe her anxiety.

"She had rheumatism all over her body. It wasn't quite like this.

JENNIFER YOUNGBLOOD & CRAIG DEPEW, MD

She didn't have such a rash. She caught emphysema when she was about fifty and went downhill pretty fast. She only lasted until she was about fifty-six."

"And how was she related to you?" asked Sam.

"My sister's girl," Douglas explained.

Sam pulled a pad from his desk drawer and started scribbling. "I'd like you to start seeing the physical therapist. You're welcome to go over to Daphne next to the hospital, but it might be easier if you see the one who comes here to my office on Wednesdays and Fridays. I think they can help a lot with the joint and muscle pain. Prednisone helped, but it's not a medicine I can keep you on for a long time, at least not for this. I'm going to give you a prescription for methotrexate. It's fairly toxic stuff so I'll need to have you come back once a month for the first little while and get blood tests to make sure I'm not killing you with it. I'm going to have Jan take a chest X-ray today. We can get this under control, Douglas, but it won't be easy."

Harper sighed, her expression relaxing a fraction.

Douglas heaved out a heavy breath. "I thought not, but let's do what we can."

They stood in unison. Sam opened the door for them. Harper waited respectfully for Douglas to leave, conveniently close enough to Sam that she placed her hand on top of his while he held the doorknob without her grandfather seeing the gesture. Awareness shot up his arm at her warm, soft touch.

"For what it's worth, thanks." A brief smile curved her lips, and he thought he caught a flicker of something in her eyes that let him know there was still hope for them.

Before Sam could articulate a response, Harper followed Douglas out the door. "Grandpa, can you handle the X-ray all by yourself?" she asked.

Douglas grunted something, and she walked out the front door. Sam instantly felt the loss of her presence.

Sam went to his next patient, his mind ran through the meeting with Harper. Was she warming up to him or had she merely been polite? He wrote a prescription for birth control pills for Sandy Van

Morrison and told her to come back before too long for her exam. When he came out of the room, Douglas Foster stood waiting with Jan. "Can I ask you one more question, doc?"

"Certainly. Step into this room." Sam closed the door behind them.

"I read about that picnic you had with Pepper McClain." A deep furrow creased his brows. "I want you to know that you hurt Harper bad." He flung Sam a scorching look. "What happened to all that talk about you being sweet on Harper? You were gonna give her time to work through her past hurts." His jaw hardened. "I don't take kindly to people hurting my girls. I'm not threatening or nothing, but I want you to know I'm watching you."

Sam weighed his words before answering. "The VC were famous for ambushing our soldiers in Vietnam. Did that ever happen to you?"

He rubbed his jaw thoughtfully. "Yeah, it did. We lost plenty of good men that way. Of course, they lost a lot more than we did."

"Pepper ambushed me that day. I never saw it coming. By the time I realized what was going on I'd already stepped on a landmine. There was no backing out. The only way out of it was forward."

"You know people around here swear by that web newspaper thing Maryanne Wheatley writes. It almost doesn't matter if you're telling me the truth. This is going to be a hard thing to live down."

"I understand. I also think it doesn't matter what everyone else thinks. The only person whose opinion I need to worry about is Harper's." He cleared his throat. "Well, maybe I should also worry about yours."

"You certainly should," Douglas said. Sam looked for a wink and a grin from the old man but there were none.

CHAPTER 14

*S*eeing Sam this morning at the clinic jolted Harper making it nearly impossible for her to stay focused on work. As more and more time passed, Harper wondered if she'd been too quick to judge Sam. After all, the proof was in the pudding. To Harper's knowledge, Sam hadn't had any dealings with Pepper since the picnic. Had they been dating, Harper was sure she would've caught wind of something through the Clementine grapevine.

Sam was so adamant about denying any feelings for Pepper. On the other hand, he had stuck around to have dinner with Pepper. And, he did kiss Pepper ... err, vice versa. Thinking about Sam kissing another woman still boiled Harper's blood. Pepper was one of the most conniving women on the planet, but Sam hadn't lived in Clementine long enough to realize that. While Harper's head knew it wasn't fair to punish Sam for Warner's betrayal, her heart had other ideas. Harper wanted to trust Sam. Seeing the compassionate way he'd dealt with Grandpa Douglas had been touching. Sam cared about his patients. Was it possible to put the unpleasantness behind them and start over?

Placing her hand over Sam's was a spontaneous gesture brought on by appreciation for how well Sam was caring for Grandpa

Douglas. Harper had been on the phone with Scarlett several times, discussing Grandpa Douglas's wellbeing. It was hard for them both to come to grips with the fact that their larger-than-life hero was growing old. Harper was grateful Grandpa had Coralee in his life. Harper suspected their close relationship was one of the things keeping him spry.

Suddenly, Harper realized she wasn't any different from Grandpa Douglas. Before Sam had come along, Harper was content with her life, telling herself that running the restaurant was enough to keep her fulfilled. Now, she knew that was a lie. Sam had brought zest into her life. Without him, life was colorless and drab. But, could she trust him? A chill ran down her spine. Trust meant everything to Harper. Her thoughts were so muddled it was hard to make sense of them. Harper's mind told her to move on. Today, however, the beseeching expression on Sam's handsome face had tugged at her heartstrings, making her question if she should welcome him back into her life ... or at least let him ease back in gradually.

Her workers were her best friends. More than employees, they came in early and left late. During those hours without customers they all talked together. They shared joys, sorrows, hopes, disappointments, and successes. It was no surprise that they all had advice for Harper. "Get rid of him," Andi said. "If my boyfriend followed a note on his windshield, he'd be in the doghouse until I forgot who he was. He knows I'd never leave notes for him."

"He truly thought you were waiting for him at that park," another one said. "It's just sweet that he went looking for you. The fact that it wasn't you has nothing to do with his feelings or intentions."

"Doctors are beasts. Go find a nice accountant," advised her kitchen supervisor.

Even the busboy chimed in. "My girlfriend is still mad over the picture in the yearbook of me and my prom date. High school ended six months ago. She needs to just get over it. Maybe you should give Sam a chance."

Frank the head cook had lived in Clementine his entire life. What gave him sage wisdom was the fact that he'd been faithfully, or as he put it *successfully*, married for thirty-six years. "It was an innocent mistake, Harper. No, it wasn't even a mistake on Sam's part. He was victimized, same as you. Take it as something you went through together, and let it make you stronger together."

Frank's advice swirled through Harper's mind. Her office window gave her a bird's-eye view of Sam's clinic. The past week and a half since she and Sam had been apart, Harper spent more time in her office, especially in the mornings and evenings when she had a greater chance of getting a glimpse of Sam's comings and goings.

A few minutes later, Sam stepped out of the clinic and locked the door behind him. Felicia and Jan had left a few minutes earlier, so Harper knew it wouldn't be long before Sam emerged to go home for the day.

Warmth started in her chest, spread down to her belly and up into her neck. She sucked in a breath. Sam's military-broad shoulders, healing hands, tanned face, and everything about him was just right. He was a compassionate servant of the sick, a selfless giver of his time and talents. What could make a man more attractive than that? He could have put himself up as more talented and educated than everyone else in this town. Yet in his spare time he liked to simply drive his old tractor around his gentleman's farm.

Harper snapped out of her reverie. She had work to do. The bills in front of her wouldn't pay themselves. She picked up one from Mr. Evans, south of town. It was for four hundred pounds of sweet potatoes. That was a lot of potatoes, but since they went into her signature pie she needed a lot. Sam sure liked her pie.

She shook her head back and forth. The paperwork in front of her demanded attention. It was like a mean, old school teacher slapping her knuckles every time her mind wandered. She had to focus. She had a business to run, customers to feed, and employees to support. She couldn't keep thinking about Sam. *Oh, Sam! How did we get here?* Maybe she should give him another chance.

Andi stepped into the office and glanced at the window. "The doc already leave for the day?"

Harper rocked back blinking several times. "How should I know?"

Andi sat down in a chair across from Harper's desk. "Maybe because you've been disappearing every evening, so you can watch him leave his office"

Heat flamed Harper's face. "Is it that obvious?" she groaned.

"Just to me," Andi chuckled.

Harper looked down at her hands. "All right, I admit it. I miss him." She braced herself for the lecture she was sure to get from Andi—the one about how Harper should lock her heart and move on. She was surprised, however, when she looked up and realized Andi was smiling.

"What?" Andi was a year and a few months younger than Harper. Andi had dated a lot of guys, and she wasn't one to take any crap.

"I know I told you that Sam was a scumbag, but I'm starting to question that assumption."

Harper jerked. "Really?"

"Yeah, the more I've thought about it, the more I'm starting to think that Sam was set up."

"What makes you say that?"

"Well, for starters, I ran into Felicia at the grocery store the other day, and she said that Sam has been miserable without you."

Harper couldn't stop a broad smile from spilling over her lips. "Really?"

"Yep. And according to Felicia, Sam told her the same thing he told you—that he was set up." Andi raised her eyebrows, wrinkling her forehead. "That still doesn't excuse the doc for being stupid when it comes to the wiles of the opposite sex."

Harper laughed, feeling some of the tension inside of her release. A few moments later, she looked at Andi. "Do you think I should give Sam another chance?"

Andi spread her hands. "That's up to you."

"I want to," Harper said carefully.

Andi gave her a searching look. "But?"

"But, a part of me is afraid."

"That's normal." Andi leaned forward. "You could test the waters."

Harper was intrigued. "What do you mean?"

"Well, you could start dating again, but just go slow. There's no rush."

"That was my thought from the get-go, but Sam wanted to sprint to the altar." She shifted in her seat. "In fact, there's this tiny part of me that wonders if maybe Sam got tired of waiting around, and that's the real reason he stayed for the picnic with Pepper. You're the one who told me to stop playing games or else I'd lose Sam."

Andi made a face. "I guess I did say that, didn't I?" She paused, looking thoughtful. "I was mainly concerned that you were dwelling too much on what happened with Warner and that it was preventing you from making a commitment to Sam."

Harper let out a humorless laugh. "Ironic, isn't it? I thought I was over the moon for Warner, but now, I realize that I didn't have a clue what it meant to love someone with your whole heart and soul … until now." Moisture rose in her eyes. "You have no idea how much I want Sam to be my knight in shining armor. I want him to be the man he appears to be."

"It's looking more and more like he is."

"It is, isn't it?" Harper felt like a ray of sunlight had pierced the gloom of the leaden clouds.

"Considering all that's happened, I do think it's in your best interest to proceed with caution," Andi warned.

"Absolutely," Harper boomed. A new determination trickled through her veins. With that came a tingle of excitement. She would give Sam another chance.

And, this time, she wasn't about to let Pepper McClain mess it up!

CHAPTER 15

*J*an walked into the office looking concerned. Sam looked up at her from the journal article he was reading. "Morning. Is everything okay?"

"Did you see the news? There's a Cat Five brewing down off the west side of Cuba. They say it's coming around and is going to head straight for us."

"You forget. I'm from New Jersey. What's a Cat Five?"

"A hurricane. A big one. Category Five is the worst."

"Oh. All right, we'll lock all the windows and it should be okay."

Felicia snickered under her breath. "Really, doc? Lock the windows? We're far enough inland that we won't get the biggest impact, but we'll still get hit. Most people leave town. You might want to leave too."

"We get some pretty good nor'easters back home. This can't be any worse than those."

She arched an eyebrow. "Wanna bet? This one comes with a storm surge, ten feet of ocean water pushed by the storm up onto the coast. Then, as the hurricane moves inland toward us it starts spinning off tornadoes. You don't want to stick around."

"We may not get the storm surge," Felicia chimed in, "but we get flooded. I remember when Irma came through back in '17. The ground got saturated after the first three hours and couldn't soak up any more rain. We ended up with four feet of standing water."

Sam put the journal article aside, removed his feet from his desk, and sat up in his seat. "Wow. That sounds serious. Where do you go for shelter?"

"Lots of people go to Birmingham," Jan answered. "It's only four hours away."

He sighed. "I guess I should look into making a hotel reservation. Have you guys already made your reservations?"

A look passed between Felicia and Jan.

"What?" Sam asked.

Jan offered a sheepish grin. "We don't usually leave."

"We prefer to just tough it out and stay in our own homes," Felicia piped in. "Fighting the long line of snail-like traffic is worse than the storm."

Sam laughed. "I see how it is. You guys have no problem toughing it out, but you think I'm a wimp."

Color seeped into Felicia's round cheeks as she chuckled. "Well, you're not from here, so you don't know what to expect."

He pulled a face. "I'm tougher than I look. I've braved many a dust storm in Afghanistan."

Jan giggled as she looked at Felicia. "It's a good thing the doc thinks he's tough, because he'll need all the torque he can muster to get through his first patient."

"That's the truth," Felicia agreed wide-eyed.

"Who's my first patient?" Sam asked, concern seeping through him.

"Mrs. Hankins," Felicia answered. "She's a doozy."

"Mrs. Hankins has been picking fine red and blue fibers out of her skin. She wants you to get rid of them."

"Yeah, she wants you to rid her of the fibers and the voices that have been telling her what to do for the last twenty years," added Jan.

Sam pursed his lips. "You know, she really doesn't sound like a surgical patient to me."

"She isn't, but you're the only person in town with M. D. after his name, so you get all comers."

Sam rolled his eyes. "Gee, thanks."

Felicia and Jan left Sam's office. He turned on the computer to review the lab reports that had come in overnight. Felicia had already forwarded several phone messages to his inbox. Once the morning housekeeping tasks were done, he leaned back in his chair and looked out the window at The Magnolia. Sam was still trying to come up with some grand gesture that would help him get back in Harper's good graces. Maybe he should start with buying her flowers. Harper loved flowers. Sam couldn't stand sitting back and doing nothing. Okay, it was settled. He'd take Harper flowers today. Maybe he'd also throw in a box of chocolate for good measure.

A second later, Jan stuck her head in the doorway, her eyes holding a mischievous twinkle. "Mrs. Hankins is ready."

"Better get to work then," Sam said as he heaved himself up by the armrests and began his day. As his staff promised, the appointment with Mrs. Hankins was something for the books. Sam felt for the poor woman who believed to the depth of her soul that aliens had implanted fibers in her skin to use as some sort of control mechanism. Needless to say, he spent far more time than scheduled with his first patient but was able to catch up by making quick work of two ingrown toenails on the high school basketball center. He treated a few diabetics, refilled blood pressure pills, took care of Mrs. Johnson's early mild pneumonia, and injected Mr. Albers' arthritic knees. Al Bluffton had acquired a Morton's neuroma during his stint in the Navy that made him feel like he had a constant pebble in his shoe. Sam carved it out of his foot right before lunch.

Felicia and Jan met him at the door of his office. "What's on the menu today, boss?"

"I brought a sandwich from home."

Silent information passed between the women before Felicia

spoke. "We've been watching you for days. Jan and I can't stand to see you moping around like this. It's time you went to see Harper again."

"I'm not moping," he grumbled.

"If you have to say it … it probably ain't true," Jan retorted, wagging her finger. "You're dealing with two grown women here, and between us, we've helped over half a dozen grown kids survive more breakups and makeups than we care to think about. We know mopey when we see it. You're mopey."

Felicia picked up where Jan left off. "It's obvious that you've got feelings for Harper, and everyone in town knows she has feelings for you. Quit stalling. You've faced off with bombers trying to kill you, for Pete's sake. This situation is a lot less dangerous than that." She grimaced. "I think."

"It is Harper Boyce he's dealing with," Felicia inserted. "That one's saucy." Admiration coated her voice.

Jan paddled her hand in a circular motion. "Now man up and get moving. Your sandwich will still be here tomorrow."

The corners of Sam's lips twitched in amusement. "Yeah, but the lettuce will be all wilted and gross."

Felicia looked him in the eye. "I know you care about Harper. She's hurting too, probably more than you are. If you don't love yourself enough to take care of this, do it for her sake. Go over there and at least find out where things stand."

"We'll eat the sandwich for you," Jan volunteered.

Sam pushed out a long breath. "I know, you're right. I wasn't really looking forward to the sandwich anyway." He set down his stethoscope and started walking to the front door. Felicia and Jan followed on his heels. Just before going out the front door, he paused and looked back. "I didn't know I'd hired a couple of matchmakers." He gave them an appreciative look. "But, I'm glad I did."

Felicia and Jan just grinned.

Andi was not nearly as icy when Sam walked through the door of the restaurant. That was a good sign. "Hiya, doc."

"Hey."

A teasing glint lit her eyes. "So, did you come for lunch, or something more?"

Sam pursed his lips. "Maybe I'll do lunch first. Get my last meal in before walking the green mile."

Andi chuckled. "Smart man." Andi motioned with her head. "Right this way." She led him to a table near the kitchen, and instead of going straight back to her hosting stand, she walked into the kitchen. Sam wondered if she was going to tell Harper he was here.

Sam scanned the menu. Marie came over wearing a large smile. "Dr. Wallentine, good to see you back. What'll it be? Our special today's shrimp and grits."

"Do you really put shrimp in grits?" he teased.

Her hand went to her hip. "You've never had it?"

"The only times I've had grits were in the Army. Some mornings the powdered eggs were just too rubbery. But with enough syrup you can eat anything, even boiled cornmeal."

Marie was aghast. "You put syrup on grits? That's disgusting."

This time, Sam was serious. He assumed everyone put either sugar or syrup on grits. "What do you put on them?"

"Butter and pepper, of course, like a normal person. You'll love ours. Shrimp, parmesan cheese, a touch of sausage grease. They're perfect."

Sam closed the menu. "You talked me into it. Sounds like an atherosclerotic feast."

A puzzled look crossed Marie's face. "A what?"

"It probably has enough sodium and cholesterol to push me five steps closer to a heart attack," he explained.

Marie grinned in understanding. "All the good stuff does, you know." She walked Sam's order into the kitchen.

Ten minutes later, as he gazed out the window at the stringy wisps of clouds on the southern horizon wondering if the approaching storm would be as bad as Felicia and Jan had predicted, there was a clink on his table. Sam turned around pleased to see Harper standing there. She placed his grits and toast in front of him. "Your last meal, sir."

He chuckled. "I see you've been talking to Andi."

"News travels fast around here. I see you're branching out from grilled cheese today." There was a hint of a smile on her face.

"I'm living dangerously," he quipped, enjoying the swift spark of connection joining them. Was it possible that the tide was starting to turn in his favor?

Harper pulled out a chair and sat down.

For a second, Sam was afraid to speak for fear of breaking the spell. Something big was brewing. He felt every eye in the place watching him. The cooks even peered out through the kitchen doorway.

"You look great."

"Thanks," she murmured as she looked down at herself, a faint rose blush coming into her cheeks. He traced the lines of her milky neck, thinking how Harper was the perfect combination of refinement and spunkiness. The pink fabric of her blouse brought out the hint of Irish red in her soft, blonde hair, framing her face just right.

She motioned. "Go ahead and eat."

Eating was the last thing on Sam's mind right now, but he picked up his fork and took a bite.

She gave him an expectant look. "How is it?"

Sam kept a straight face. "Not bad." It was cute the way her eyebrow arched. "It would be better with some syrup … for the grits."

She smirked. "Spoken like a Yankee."

A playful grin tugged at his lips as he leaned forward, lowering his voice. "Admit it, you have a thing for Yankees."

Her eyes rounded as she laughed in surprise. "Just New Jersey boys."

Their gazes locked. Sam felt his blood run faster. "I've missed you."

"I've missed you, too."

Sam peered into Harper's magnetic eyes, glistening sapphire blue with flakes of gold. A touch of moisture sparkled around the edges.

"Can we start over?" Harper asked, her voice was soft and imploring.

His heart leapt with anticipation. "I'd like that."

"Slowly," she cautioned.

He swallowed, feeling as though he was holding a rare butterfly in his hand. The trick was to keep her at ease so she wouldn't fly away. Suddenly, Sam knew what his grand gesture needed to be. "Why don't you come over tonight? I'll make you dinner."

Amusement flickered across Harper's features. "What's on the menu?"

Sam was a decent cook, but nothing compared to Harper. "Hmm … let's see, I make a mean peanut butter and banana sandwich." He chuckled at the mortified look on Harper's face. He winked. "I might be able to scrounge up something a little fancier than that for the chef."

She shook her head back and forth. "I wish I could, but I have to work late tonight."

His stomach dropped.

Her voice lifted. "But, I can come tomorrow night."

He smiled. "Sounds good to me."

She frowned. "Wait, that might not work."

Disappointment lodged in his throat. This was worse than a roller coaster ride. "Why not?"

"There's supposed to be a bad storm coming."

"The Cat Five."

"Yes," she said, looking impressed that he knew the lingo.

"Well, you could come over early. When the storm hits, we'll weather it together. Whaddaya say, Alabama girl? You willing to brave the storm with this here Yankee?"

She laughed. "Now, that's living dangerously," she uttered in a husky drawl that sent shivers of anticipation racing through him.

He held his breath waiting for her answer.

"Okay, you talked me into it, Mr. New Jersey." She scooted back her chair and stood. "Tomorrow night." There was a hint of promise in her eyes.

"Tomorrow night," he reiterated with conviction.

She motioned. "Better eat those grits while they're hot. Otherwise, you will need syrup to choke them down. See ya, New Jersey," she quipped with a wink.

Sam watched Harper glide away, her hips making a soft, swaying motion. She was a vision, the most intoxicating woman he'd ever been around. He glanced up at the ceiling and offered a quick, silent prayer of thanks that he'd been given a second chance. This time, he was determined to do things right!

CHAPTER 16

*S*am locked the door of the clinic and glanced up at the sky. Due to the approaching storm, he closed shop early today and got no complaints from Felicia or Jan. The air was eerily calm, giving Sam the feeling energy was building like a giant fist drawing back, getting ready to strike. He made a quick run to the grocery store to pick up items for dinner. The stop ended up taking longer than he thought because three quarters of the town was there buying staples. Many shelves were already empty, but Sam managed to snag some ground beef and the last package of hamburger buns.

As the sales clerk rang up his groceries, she chattered excitedly about the impending storm and how crazy it had been at the store. Then, she asked Sam if he'd heard the news about the notorious criminals that had been lurking around Clementine. Before Sam could get a word in edgewise, the young girl rushed on.

"Judd Barber and Peter Morrison robbed a convenience store this morning on the outskirts of town. They shot the attendant in the shoulder. As the man went down, he grabbed a pistol from underneath the counter and fired back, injuring Judd Barber. There's a manhunt underway for them. I just hope the law catches them before the storm hits. That's rotten timing."

As if there ever were a good time for a robbery and shootings to occur. Sam had come to Clementine looking for a respite from the violence he'd experienced in the military. And yet, there seemed to be no escaping it, even here in quaint Clementine. He was grateful that he'd installed the alarm on his building. Although, he'd not seen any evidence of the men lurking around. Maybe their intent to break into his clinic was a passing fancy. They'd moved onto bigger targets, obviously.

When Sam arrived home, he did a quick sweep to clean everything up. According to the National Weather Service, the storm was set to hit around eight p.m. The plan was for Harper to arrive at five. It was a little after one p.m. Provided the weather held, Sam planned to piddle around in his yard and garden for a couple hours, and then get a shower. He was serving hamburgers, baked beans, and potato chips for dinner. Not a gourmet meal Harper was famous for, but it would be tasty. His original plan had been to get a pie or cake at the grocery store bakery, but they were all gone. He opted for a half gallon of ice cream instead. Thankfully, there were still plenty of bouquets left. He'd picked the largest one and found a box of chocolate.

By the time five o'clock rolled around, Sam was about midway done with preparing dinner. The beans were in the oven, and he'd made the patties. He still needed to pan fry them. He'd been meaning to get a grill but hadn't gotten around to it yet. On a night like tonight, a grill was a moot point because he and Harper would stay indoors. Sam's thoughts went back to his garden. He'd gotten a lot done in a short amount of time. The weather was still clear, but the wind was starting to pick up. He wanted Harper to get here soon, not just because he was craving her company, but also because he didn't want her on the road during the storm. A few minutes later, the doorbell rang, sending a rush of anticipation through him.

He went to get it. "Hello," he said with a large smile when he opened the door.

"Hello," Harper repeated as she held up a round covered dish. "I brought a peace offering in the way of sweet potato pie." There was a hint of shyness in Harper's demeanor, letting Sam know she wasn't sure how to navigate their reconciliation.

"You're bringing out the big gun now," Sam teased. He could tell that the joke helped ease Harper's nerves. He stepped back. "Come on in." As she stepped past him, he caught the faint floral scent of her cologne. Her glossy hair seemed to collect the light in the foyer as it bounced softly on her shoulders. Sam had to fight the temptation to pull her into his arms for a long kiss. He was grateful that Harper was here and had to remind himself to proceed cautiously; so as not to scare the rare butterfly away. An unexpected sting stabbed through him. Sam didn't want to start over again as polite strangers. He wanted to fast forward to where they'd been before. Hopefully, dinner would help buff off any residual hard feelings or misunderstandings. He and Harper still needed to talk about what happened, but that could wait until they were both more relaxed.

"How was the weather coming over?" Sam asked as Harper set the pie down on the counter. She slid the strap off her shoulder and tucked her purse into the counter space beside the refrigerator.

"Still pretty calm, but I get the feeling that we're gonna be in for it. Grandpa Douglas came over to the restaurant and boarded up the windows."

The corners of Sam's lips pulled down. "You should've told me. I would've helped." Maybe he should've considered boarding up the windows of his clinic.

She waved a hand. "Nah, he took care of it just fine." Her lips twitched. "I figured you had enough on your plate today with this." She motioned to the food.

"Yep, these burgers and baked beans have pushed me to the limit," he said solemnly, fighting the urge to break into a grin.

Harper chuckled. "What? No grilled cheese?" She clucked her tongue. "I'm disappointed."

"Oh, no. I wouldn't dare attempt to make the chef grilled cheese sandwiches. Anything I did would pale in comparison to the expert."

She grunted, but Sam could tell from her begrudging smile that Harper was pleased with his compliment. "What can I do to help?"

"No cooking for you tonight. You're off duty."

Sam's kitchen was an open-style that flowed into the living room. Harper glanced in the direction of the dining room table doing a double-take when she saw the elaborately set table complete with tall candles and the flowers in the center. "Wow," she uttered, "I'm impressed." She walked over and inspected the place settings. "You even positioned the silverware correctly."

A crooked grin tugged at his lips. "It's amazing what you can learn on YouTube."

"Evidently," she laughed. "Emily Post 101."

Within a few minutes everything was ready. They carried dishes of food to the dining room.

"It seems that the doc can cook," she teased.

"You'd better reserve judgment until after you taste it."

She was about to pull out her chair, but he stopped her. "Allow me," he said as he helped her get seated. When he sat down, his knee bumped hers. A look passed between them and, reflected in her deep sapphire eyes, he thought he detected the same longing that he felt. A surge of chemistry ran through him.

"Thanks for braving the storm and coming here."

She chuckled. "Thanks for braving me." The unconscious smile that curved her lips was so captivating that it caused his heart to skip a beat.

"It's a tough job, but somebody's gotta do it."

Her smile widened. "I'm glad it's you."

He wanted to kiss her so badly at this moment that he could hardly contain himself. "Shall we pray?" he asked instead.

"I'd like that," Harper said like she was genuinely impressed that he'd suggested it.

In a swift movement, he reached over and took her hand. A current surged through him when their skin connected. He bowed his head and offered the prayer, asking for special protection from the storm. The entire time, Sam was keenly aware of her warmth seeping into him. When the prayer was over, he reluctantly released her hand.

He watched with trepidation as Harper took her first bite. "What do you think?"

After chewing and swallowing, she tipped her head in concentration. "You know," she said thoughtfully. "It's …" A large smile filled her face. "It's delicious."

"Thank you," he said happily, taking a bite of his burger. A second later, he groaned. "Ah, man!"

She grew puzzled. "What?"

"You were just being nice. The burgers are dry," he lamented.

She grinned sheepishly, color seeping into her cheeks. "I think they're good."

"Liar."

She wrinkled her nose, her eyes dancing with amusement. "They might be a tad bit dry, but they're still good. It's the effort that counts, right?"

He grunted. "That's what everyone says to the losers." Her warm laughter was infectious as Sam laughed too.

"Now, Doctor Wallentine," she chided, "you can't corner the market on all the abilities." She took a bite of the baked beans. "These really are terrific. What's your secret?"

He wagged a finger. "Oh, no, I don't give away my recipes."

"Now, you're starting to sound like an old Southern woman."

"They don't like sharing recipes?"

A velvety laugh rumbled in her throat. "Oh, no. If you press them, they'll give you a recipe, but you can't guarantee that a few of the key ingredients won't be left out."

"That's terrible," he chuckled, "but funny."

Harper made a face. "You say that, but it's not funny when you're fifteen years old trying to make a birthday cake for your grandfather, and the chocolate cake recipe that Lindy Milton shared with you won't rise."

He shook his head. "Did you have to go buy one?" He took a bite of the beans and chewed appreciatively. Harper was right. They were superb.

"No, thankfully, Ninny Halstrom lived only a few doors down.

Grandpa Douglas called her to come over and help, since I was having a breakdown. It turned out to be a great blessing because Ninny took me and Scarlett under her wing and taught us how to cook."

Sam searched his memory. "I don't believe I've met Ninny Halstrom."

Harper's expression grew wistful. "No, you wouldn't have met her. She passed away when I was nineteen."

"I'm sorry," Sam said automatically.

"Thanks, but it was a long time ago. Now, I just remember all the wonderful times we had together."

"Ninny ... that's an unusual name."

Harper had just taken a large bite of her burger. She chewed quickly and took a sip of lemonade. "Her real name was Mildred. Ninny was a nickname."

"Oh? for what?"

She chuckled like she couldn't believe he'd asked such a question. "Grandmom." She shook her head. "I can't believe you've never heard that term before."

"Never."

Harper cleared her throat and said in her best New Jersey accent. "Oh, forgive me. In your neck of the woods, the correct term would be grandmother."

"Nope, not even close."

Her forehead crinkled. "Grandma?"

He shook his head in the negative.

"Yaya, Mimi?"

A smile tugged at his lips. "Granz."

Her eyebrow lifted. "Granz, that's sophisticated."

"Yes, she was quite the woman. She died a few years ago." He grew reflective. "I still miss her."

Harper nodded, a flash of sympathy in her eyes.

"Granz loved to cook. There was this one Christmas dinner when she fed the whole family; us, the cousins, the mailman, everybody. I was seven or eight years old. They called on my big sister to say the prayer for the meal. She said, 'God bless this juicy meat that Granz made. God bless the rolls Granz made. God bless the mashed pota-toes. God bless the gravy. God bless the juice. God bless the beans.' And on and on and on. It was just annoying. I was starved. Finally, when she got to the chocolate cake, I couldn't handle it a minute longer. I screamed out, 'God bless Betty Crocker, Amen!'"

Harper's eyes popped the second before peals of laughter erupted from her lips. A second later, she reached for her napkin and dabbed the corners of her eyes. "I'll bet you were a handful."

"According to my mother, I was." He flashed a grin. "She always says she hopes I have one just like me."

Harper shook her head. "That would be poetic justice, I suppose."

The hiss of the wind sounded from outside, followed by pelting rain.

"It sounds like the storm's here," Harper said.

Sam got up from the table, went to the window, and pushed aside the blinds. He was surprised by how dark the sky had become. The wind was raging, sending rain slicing sideways through the air. He glanced back at Harper who wore a look of concern. "That came on fast," he observed.

Harper put down her fork. "Welcome to the Gulf Coast."

"Can't be worse than a dust storm in Afghanistan," Sam said stubbornly.

"Don't be too sure."

A sense of foreboding slithered down Sam's spine as he looked at the giant oak tree on the far edge of his garden. The normally sturdy, steadfast limbs were writhing like pipe cleaners, and the storm was only getting started. His garbage can went sailing by, tumbling haphazardly. The wind ripped a plank from the picket fence and slung it against the house with a large pop.

A surprised yelp escaped Harper's lips. "That scared me," she said, as if talking to herself. She rose from her chair, hugging her arms. "Maybe you should back away from the window ... just in case."

"Good idea," Sam said as he stepped back.

The roof sounded like it was under siege, and the windows rattled, trying to withstand the onslaught of wind and rain.

They stood for a minute looking at each other. "Should we continue eating?" Sam asked. "I'm sure we'll be okay inside."

Harper hesitated. "Sure," she finally said.

They sat back down and went through the motions of finishing dinner, even though their thoughts were on the storm. Every time they heard a loud pop against the house, Harper flinched. Sam assumed the sound was planks from his fence. He didn't even want to think about the havoc being wreaked on his garden and yard, not mention his house. "Douglas was smart to board up the windows on the restaurant."

"Yes, he was," Harper agreed. "I probably should've asked him to board up the windows on my house."

"I'm with you. I should've done that too."

The lights flickered.

"Do you have emergency candles?" Her voice was laced with tension.

"Yep, sure do," Sam said with a touch of pride that he was so prepared. "On the counter in the kitchen."

"Good," she sighed, "we might need them."

He pumped his eyebrows, a sense of adventure trickling through him. "I can think of worse things than being stuck in the dark with you."

She chuckled. "Hah, you're funny," she retorted, but the worry lines eased from her face, her shoulders relaxing a fraction.

Thirty minutes later, the storm stopped as suddenly as it had begun.

Sam breathed a sigh of relief as he offered a reassuring smile. "That wasn't too bad. We didn't even lose power."

"Yep, and no windows were broken."

He stood and peered out the window. His heart sank as he surveyed the damage. Even in the dimness of the single light on the back of the house, Sam could tell that his yard and garden looked like a war zone. His crops were bent to the ground, and there were gaps in the fence, reminding him of missing teeth.

Harper came up beside him and put a hand on his arm. "All your hard work. I'm sorry."

"Well, it could've been worse," he said with a resigned sigh.

Her lips formed grim lines as her head slowly swung back and forth. "It's probably not over."

He stiffened. "Huh?"

"Hurricanes aren't always big circular blobs. Sometimes they have arms radiating out. One must have just passed over us. I suspect there will be another wave soon. I can check the weather on my phone."

"Or, we could go over to the couch and turn on the TV," he suggested.

"Good idea."

When they sat down, Sam was pleased when Harper scooted close to him. After turning to the weather channel, he draped an arm around her shoulders. She snuggled into the curve of his arm. He allowed himself a moment to soak in being this close to Harper before turning his attention to The Weather Channel. With a solemn expression, the anchorman confirmed what Harper had suspected—another wave was on the way. Sam didn't like the feeling of being a sitting duck.

The lights flickered.

"Uh, oh," Harper said as the power went out, plunging them into darkness.

Sam hoped the power might come back on, but it didn't. "You stay here, and I'll get a candle." Cautiously, he made his way to the kitchen, feeling his way as he went. He'd left his phone on the counter beside the candles. He reached for it first, turning on the flashlight. He shined it in Harper's direction. "You okay?"

"I'm good." Quickly, she stood and came toward him.

He handed her his phone. "Would you mind holding this while I light the candle?" The candle was the chunky kind, about five inches in diameter, but still easily held in the palm of the hand.

"Sure."

He struck the match and put it to the candlewick. A soft halo of light dispelled the darkness, making Sam feel better about the situation.

A loud knock sounded at the door. Sam and Harper both jumped simultaneously.

Harper's eyes widened as she clutched his phone with both hands. "Are you expecting anyone?"

"No."

There was a cluster of insistent knocks like knuckles rapping against the door. "Someone may need help." If his garden and yard were any indication of the damage, roads were probably just as bad.

Harper offered a slight smile. "Well, they came to the right place." A shudder ran through her as she cast him a grateful look, a wan smile touching her lips. "I'm glad I'm here with you instead of home alone."

Her confidence in him was reassuring, but Sam could tell from her expression that she was trying to say something more. The inference was that she wanted to be here with him, and not just because of the storm. Hope kindled inside him. The evening was going much better than he hoped despite the storm. They shared a smile. "Thank you." He couldn't help it. The temptation to touch her cheek was too great.

She stepped closer, peering into his eyes. "Sam," she uttered, her lips parting.

A jolt raced through his veins as he leaned in to kiss her. He stopped short at the loud knocking. "Sheesh, already. I'm coming," he grumbled.

She laughed, playfully pushing his arm. "Go on." There was an expression of promise in her beautiful eyes. Then, a wry grin touched her lips. "There'll be plenty of time later to continue this discussion."

A deep chuckle rumbled in his throat as he touched her lips with the tip of his finger. "This is a conversation I look forward to having." There was a spring in his step as he went to the door, his hand cradling the candle as he held it in front of him. Before Sam even got to the living room, the door burst open. Two drenched men stumbled inside. One of the men kicked the door closed with his heel.

"What the—!" Sam's next word was cut off when he saw the flash of metal and realized the man bracing the other had a gun.

CHAPTER 17

Sam took a quick snapshot of the intruders. One man had his arm slung around the other's shoulders, and he was pressing what looked to be a t-shirt to his abdomen with his free hand. The wad of fabric was soaked in blood, and there was a large, expanding circle of red on the man's shirt beneath his hand. His breathing was raspy and labored. Instinctively, Sam stepped back needing to get to Harper, so he could protect her.

"Don't move!" the man shouted, aiming the gun at Sam. There was a crazy, desperate look in the man's eyes. "Easy," Sam said, his military instincts taking hold as his muscles pulled taut, preparing to spring into action. Sam kept a gun in his safe in the bedroom closet. He just needed to figure out a way to get to it.

Sam felt movement as Harper stepped up beside him. "Stay back," Sam warned, trying to shield her with his free arm.

"Peter Morrison? Judd Barber? What're you doing here in Doctor Sam Wallentine's home?" Harper demanded in the loud, irritated tone of an older sister scolding an errant child. "Greenbrier road is a far cry from the convenience store. You must've been on the run all day long."

It went through Sam's mind that Harper was spitting out a lot of unnecessary information. Then realization punched through Sam. Harper still had his phone. He'd handed it to her before lighting the candle. Had she dialed 911 and put the phone on speaker? It was a smart move, but it could backfire if Peter realized what she was doing. Sam touched Harper's arm, trying to convey silent information for her to stop talking.

Training the gun on them, Peter inched over to the couch where he deposited Judd who moaned. Sam almost attacked Peter from behind, but Peter sprang around, wielding the gun like he'd read Sam's mind.

"It—hurts—so—bad!" Judd whined.

"I need you to patch him up, Doc," Peter said gruffly.

Sam's jaw tightened. "Gunshot wounds are nasty. He needs to get to a hospital, so he can get the proper treatment he needs." Judd had been shot this morning. He'd lost a lot of blood. It was a wonder that he was even conscious.

Peter's eyes narrowed to black slashes. "The only one who's gonna be treating anybody is you. Get to work," he barked.

The flicker of the candle cast exaggerated shadows over Peter's features, giving Sam the impression that his loose, fleshy skin might fall off his face. Sam took a quick mental assessment. The middle-aged stocky man had the hard edge of having served time. He wasn't nervous with the gun, but held it confidently like he wasn't afraid to use it. Instinct told Sam that he could take the man in a fight. The trick was to get the pistol away from him before anyone got hurt. Peter's clothes were soaking wet, water puddling onto the floor at his feet. The beleaguered appearance of the men spoke of their day-long ordeal evading the police. Sam knew from sad experience in Afghanistan that Peter was the worst sort of man—desperate.

Harper's voice held a knife-edge as it cut through the room. "That was stupid of you and Judd to hold up a convenience store. What were you thinking?"

A sneer twisted over Peter's face. "You always did have a mouth on you, Harper." He aimed the gun at her face. "I know of one way to shut you up."

Harper gasped, shrinking back.

Sam's stomach tightened. "Easy." He stepped in front of Harper, using his body as a shield. He could feel Harper's fear spilling out and mixing with his own. In the near darkness, the situation had a horror-flick, surreal feel. Unfortunately, this wasn't something out of a movie. It was painfully real. Scenes from the blistering Afghan desert streaked through his mind. The loud crack of the explosion, the acrid smell of smoke in his nostrils, and the suffocating despair. Sam had been unable to save his friends and coworkers. So many lives lost in senseless violence. He couldn't—wouldn't—allow that to happen now. Harper was his world. He'd die trying to save her, if that's what it took. This time, he wouldn't fail.

Judd's ragged breaths filled the silence between them. There were a few intermittent whimpers. He coughed and gurgled like he was choking on his own blood.

Sam kept his voice conversational. "Sure, I'll be happy to treat Judd, but I'll need to grab my medical bag." He motioned with his head. "It's in my bedroom." Actually, Sam kept the bag in his car, but it was a good excuse to get back to the safe.

Uncertainty crept into Peter's eyes, and Sam could tell the man was trying to decide how to finagle allowing Sam to retrieve his bag while maintaining control of the situation. "There's no time to spare," Sam added, his heart thumping out a fast beat against his ribcage. *Stay calm*, he ordered himself.

"You can tell just from looking at him that he's in shock. A person who's lost this much blood won't last very long. He needs surgery and possibly a transfusion. If not, he probably has minutes to live, at best."

"My granddaddy had his appendix taken out on the kitchen table and he lived another sixty years after that. You'll do it here or else," Peter growled.

Sam looked at Harper, noticing that she kept her right hand positioned slightly behind her back. It was just as he thought. Their gazes locked, and he could tell she was trying to convey what she was doing. Her eyes were large pools of terror. "It'll be all right," he said calmly as a quiet rage ripped through his body.

"Move it! Both of you!" Peter ordered.

Stepping close and taking Harper's arm, they went down the hall. Harper shifted her right hand to her front. By this time, the 911 dispatch could surely make out what was happening. How long would it take for the police to arrive? Could they get here or had the storm rendered the roads impassable? Sam wondered why Harper didn't just end the call and place it in her pocket. Then again, any such movement could alert Peter. Maybe it was better to just keep things status quo.

As they continued toward the bedroom, Sam's skin crawled with the knowledge that Peter was close behind, holding the gun. Any false move, and he and Harper would be goners. His blood boiled and everything in him wanted to whirl around and slam Peter into the wall. Sam couldn't risk the gun going off and hitting Harper. He offered up a silent prayer, asking for help. An instant later, inspiration poured into him. It wasn't a question of whether Sam should attack but a question of when.

"It's in the closet," Sam said when they stepped into the bedroom. He held out the candle so that it would illuminate the room.

"No sudden moves," Peter growled.

Sam had the eerie impression that their shadows were dark phantoms circling around the prey. With a sinking heart, Sam realized their predicament. Peter was no intellectual by any stretch of the imagination, but the man was smart enough to see through any flimsy excuse Sam could concoct for opening the safe ... unless ... He forced his voice to sound calm. "There may be another solution to all this."

"What do you mean?" Peter muttered.

"I'm going to turn around, so we can talk."

"What're you doing?" Harper hissed.

Sam wanted to tell her to trust him, but all he could do was cast her a reassuring look.

"We're turning around," Sam said as he and Harper moved to face Peter. Sam swallowed, a sense of urgency coming over him. He got the distinct feeling that their time was running out. "Look, Judd's in bad shape. He needs to go to the hospital. There's a safe in the closet. It has cash in it. You can take that cash and run. In the meantime, I'll make sure that Judd gets the care he needs." Sam could tell that Peter was considering the offer. He held his breath, listening to the pounding rhythm of his own heart as he awaited Peter's answer.

Peter assessed him with cold snake eyes that had no compassion or feeling. "How much cash?"

Sam didn't flinch. "Ten thousand dollars." He heard Harper's soft intake of breath. She probably thought Sam was losing it, offering Peter money. It was a blatant lie. There was only a thousand dollars in the safe, but that was beside the point.

"All right," Peter said, aiming the gun at Sam. "But no funny business."

A surge of victory went through Sam. He took Harper's arm to take her with him to the closet.

"Just you," Peter ordered.

Sam reluctantly released Harper's arm. It ripped Sam to shreds to see the tight mask of worry on Harper's face. A sense of urgency over-took him with enough force to nearly steal his breath. His internal voice screamed out a warning that Sam needed to do something … fast! He took two steps toward the closet when Peter's demeanor shifted.

"What is that?" he screamed, a shrill edge of murderous hatred sounding in his voice. "You have a phone!" Swearing, Peter stepped forward and grabbed Harper. She screamed, the phone tumbling to the floor. A second later, Peter was standing behind Harper, holding her in a headlock, the gun pointed at her temple. "I should've just put a bullet in you earlier," Peter said savagely.

Sam's heart wrenched as he looked at Harper. It couldn't end like this. Not here. Not now.

Tears bubbled in Harper's eyes. "I'm sorry," she uttered.

At first, Sam thought she was apologizing for the phone.

Harper's expression was pleading as she looked at Sam. "When you told me you loved me, I was scared." Her voice trembled. "Then, when the thing with Pepper came up … well, I panicked." Her voice broke. "I should've trusted you." She sucked in a sharp breath. "You're the best thing that ever happened to me. I love you."

Everything Sam had ever wanted was right in front of him, and it was about to get ripped away by a cold, callous murderer who placed no value on other's lives, hopes, or dreams. An image of the arrogant look on the suicide bomber just before he triggered the bomb flashed through Sam's mind. *No! Not this time!* Emotion rose like a tidal wave in his chest as a sure determination swept over him. "I love you too." He locked eyes with Harper, everything in him willing her to understand the meaning of his words. "Sometimes when life comes at you unexpectedly, you have to make a dive for it."

She blinked several times, understanding registering in her eyes. Or, at least, Sam hoped she understood.

"How sweet," Peter said nastily. "Now, shut up!" he roared, yanking Harper's hair so that her head jerked back. She yelped, tears spilling down her cheeks.

Anger seared through Sam. "Let her go," he seethed. "I'll get your money, and you can be on your way."

A wild, unhinged look twisted over Peter's face, making him look more monster than human. "I'm calling the shots here," he screamed. "You got that, doc?"

"I've got it," Sam said in an even tone. Fear rose acid in his throat. He pushed it away, willing himself to keep a handle on his emotions.

From the living room, Judd started coughing. Then came guttural sounds like he was choking.

Worry streaked over Peter's features as he loosened his hold on Harper and glanced back.

"Dive!" Sam yelled as he snuffed out the candle and lunged at Peter who grunted in surprise as they toppled to the floor.

A shot sounded, and Sam felt a searing pain streak across his arm like someone had jabbed a hot poker through him. Sam used his body weight to pin Peter to the floor. Unable to see through the darkness, he felt for Peter's face. Sam pressed his thumbnails into Peter's eye sockets. The man shrieked in pain as Sam punched him in the face, again and again. Peter fought back, slinging his fists, but he was no match for Sam's military training.

A moment later, Sam heard rapid footsteps. Then, lights streaked across the room.

"Hold it right there!" a voice ordered.

Sam looked up to see two police officers, pointing guns. Grabbing Peter's shirt, Sam pulled him to his feet and handed him over to the nearest officer who handcuffed him.

"You're under arrest," the officer said brusquely as he read Peter his rights, dragging him from the room.

Sam's eyes had adjusted to the darkness. He made a frantic sweep across the room, exhaling in relief when Harper stumbled towards him and fell into his arms. He pulled her close, burying his face in her hair. "Are you okay?" he breathed.

"Yes, thanks to you," Harper answered.

An officer stepped up, shining a flashlight into their eyes. They winced at the bright light, averting their faces.

"Sorry," the officer said, lowering the flashlight to the ground. "Are y'all okay?"

"Yes," Sam answered. He rubbed a hand across Harper's back, so grateful that she was unscathed.

"Peter had a gun." Harper glanced around. "It's somewhere on the floor."

The officer nodded. "Thanks, we'll collect it as evidence."

Sam had never seen the man before, but assumed Harper knew him. Sam was surprised when Harper asked, "Where did you come from?"

For a second, the officer was confused.

"You're not from Clementine," Harper continued.

"No, we came from Daphne. There are trees down all over the highway leading out of Clementine. We could get here faster. Are you the one who called 911?"

"Yes. In fact, there's a phone around here somewhere." Harper touched Sam's arm. He grunted in pain.

"What's wrong?" Harper asked, worry coating her voice.

It occurred to Sam that his arm was throbbing. "I got shot in the arm."

Harper gasped. "Oh, no!"

Gingerly, Sam felt his arm. "I think the bullet just grazed the surface, but I won't know for sure until I can examine it in the light."

"We need to get you to a hospital," Harper said.

"Yes," the officer agreed. "My partner put in a call for an ambulance, it should be arriving soon." He paused. "Well, it may take longer than normal. The storm has started up again."

Sam cocked his ears, realizing that the wind was raging outside. "I'll be all right." Sam used his unhurt arm to encircle Harper's waist and pull her close. He wished for the light, so he could see Harper's beautiful face. "I almost lost you," he said fiercely.

"No chance of that. I meant what I said. I love you, Sam Wallentine. I want to build a life with you." She chuckled. "Heck, I even want the picket fence and houseful of rambunctious kids, even if they are little menaces like their dad."

Sam's heart leapt with anticipation, a grin tipping his lips. "I thought you wanted to take it slow."

She laughed softly. "How's this for slow?" Cupping his face in her hands, she pulled him to her and gave him a long, breathless kiss that sent a shock wave all the way from his lips to his toes, making him forget all about the pain in his arm.

EPILOGUE

*O*ne month later ...

Harper looked up as Andi waltzed into her office. Harper's eyes widened as she did a double take. "Wow, you make a convincing Wicked Witch of the West." She flashed a cheeky grin. "It must come naturally."

"Hey," Andi protested. Her face, hands, and arms were green, and she was clad from head to toe in a black gown and pointy hat.

Andi trilled out a high-pitched cackle that could've shattered glass as her fingers formed claws. "I'll get you, my pretty, and your little dog, too!"

"You do that a little too well," Harper said with a chuckle.

Andi gave Harper an appraising look. "You look great too." She frowned, "Although, with your blonde hair in braids, you look more like Daisy Mae than Dorothy."

Harper wrinkled her nose as she looked down at her blue and white gingham dress. "Yeah, I just couldn't stand the thought of wearing a wig all day." Today marked the start of the week-long Jambalaya Festival, kicking off with a parade. Harper and her group decided to do a Wizard of Oz float. Grandpa Douglas was pulling the float with his truck.

The annual festival had been taking place for decades. However, this year, it almost didn't happen because of the storm aftermath. It had taken an entire week for power to get restored. Scarlett and Rigby came into town. Harper and Scarlett provided over thirty-five hundred meals to the residents of Clementine and the surrounding areas. The cost was funded by Rigby. Harper's staff worked for free and other townspeople volunteered at the restaurant to help. The town quickly recovered, rebuilt, and restarted.

After much deliberation among town officials, it was decided that it would be beneficial for Clementine to hold the festival to unite the residents and provide a good healing balm. Mayor Tate asked Sam to serve as Grand Marshal for the parade.

"How's your man?" Andi asked.

"Good." Harper let out a long sigh.

Andi plopped down in a chair, a wrinkle forming between her brows. "What's that for? I thought things were going splendidly between you two? You've hardly spent a minute apart the past few weeks."

"Things are going great." Warmth flowed through Harper thinking of Sam. Last night, they'd spread a blanket over the grass beside his garden and gazed at the stars. Sam was such an intoxicating combination of strength and tenderness. Harper had always known that Sam was a man's man, but the night of the storm when Sam saved them, she'd seen the fierce, protective side of him. Then, he'd gazed at her with those piercing green eyes that had the power to see into her soul. His kisses ignited her with a flame of longing that grew more powerful with each passing day. Color fanned her cheeks when she realized she'd spaced out for a moment in her favorite daydream—Sam. Her brows furrowed as she tried to put her thoughts into words. "The night of the storm, when I thought I was a goner ..." The mere thought of that cold steel gun pointed at her head caused a shiver to slither down her spine. "I admitted to Sam how much I love him." She sighed, remembering. "I told him that I wanted a future with him ... a family. I assumed that we'd just pick up from there and race forward."

"But?"

She pushed out a long breath. "Well, nothing is happening." Her hands went into the air. "I mean, we're always together, and the sparks are unbelievable." Heat rose up her neck, especially when she saw Andi's deviant smile. She charged on. "I just assumed after what Sam and I went through that he would propose. Here we are a month later, and he still hasn't. At first, I thought he was holding back because of how crazy everything was with the aftermath of the storm. Now, however, things are getting back to normal and nothing." She was about to add more, but Andi's laughter cut her off short. She frowned. "What?"

Andi shook her head from side to side. "You are something else."

Irritation crawled down Harper's skin as she gave Andi a hard look. "What do you mean?"

"First, Sam tries to take the relationship to the next level and you panic, telling him you want to take things slow. Now, you're frustrated, because he isn't moving fast enough."

Harper wanted to argue, but she knew Andi had her. She wrinkled her nose, a begrudging smile tugging at her lips. "You make me sound so fickle."

Andi laughed. "Those are your words, not mine." She looked Harper in the eye. "Be patient. Give the poor guy a break. You two have been through a lot. It's not every day that a person's life flashes before their eyes."

"Amen," Harper agreed heartily. She took in a deep breath. "You're right. I need to be patient. Okay, I can do it." She wrinkled her nose. "I think."

An hour later, it was time for the parade. Harper made her way through the throng of people to the staging area where she was to meet Sam. Her heart skipped a beat when she saw him standing tall and proud in his Army Uniform. When he spotted her, a crooked grin pulled at his lips as he strode toward her, eyes flickering over her costume. "Where's Toto?" he teased as he pulled her to him and gave her a peck on the lips. Even that sent a spark tingling through her.

She gave him an appraising look. "So, Soldier Boy, you're looking mighty sharp in your uniform." Not wanting to call attention to himself, Sam had been reluctant to act as the Grand Marshal, but Mayor Tate talked him into it, telling him that as the town doctor it was up to him to take the lead in community events. Even if Sam weren't the Grand Marshal, he still would've stood out with his rugged good looks, powerful physique, and understated confidence. Sam was a born leader, and everyone but him knew it. One of the reasons she loved him so much was because of his humility.

Harper surveyed the lineup. The parade consisted of nine floats and a small marching band of kids from the middle and high school. Sam was to ride in the shiny, red Cadillac convertible at the front of the line. Harper let out a low whistle. "Wow, you're the star of the show." It tickled her to watch color rise in Sam's cheeks as he rubbed his neck.

Jeremy Rutledge a teenager who frequented The Magnolia walked up to the Cadillac. He was holding a magnetic sign. No, make that two magnetic signs. He crouched down beside the car and placed the first sign over the driver-side door. With a nimble hop, Jeremy trotted around to place the second on the passenger-side door. Harper's eyes popped as she read the sign.

She turned to Sam whose face had paled.

A fireball of indignation whirled through Harper. "Are you kidding me?" She read the sign aloud. "Grand Marshal Dr. Samuel Wallentine, Clementine Medical Care. Car sponsored by Pepper McClain, Realtor." Pepper's name was in even bigger letters than Sam's.

"I had no idea that Pepper was the sponsor," Sam said.

As if on cue, Pepper trotted up with a bouncy smile. She wore a tight white blouse, tied at the waist, and an above-the-knee denim skirt. "Hello," she said cheerfully, her eyes settling on Sam. "Looks like the two of us will be sharing a car today." She gave Harper a catty look that caused a heat wave to blast over Harper.

Sam rocked back. "That was not part of the deal."

Pepper's face fell. "What do you mean? I'm the sponsor. It's only right that I should be able to ride in the car."

Harper shook her head, disgust sitting heavy in her stomach. "You just don't give up, do you?"

"I—I don't know what you mean," Pepper blustered.

Harper leaned forward, eyeing Pepper. "Oh, I think you know exactly what I mean. You set Sam up once, but it won't happen again."

Mayor Tate stepped up. Oblivious to the drama unfolding, he began shaking hands with Sam, Harper, and Pepper. He patted Sam on the shoulder, grinning from ear to ear. "You look great, doc," he boomed,"You make our town proud."

Sam squared his jaw. "There's been a mistake. I'm not riding in a car with Pepper."

The mayor's jaw fell. "I don't understand."

Pepper's face turned tomato red. "I sponsored the car," she spat, "I have every right to ride in it."

Sam's eyes narrowed, his voice unyielding, "If you want me to be the Grand Marshal, I ride alone. If Pepper wants to ride in the car then she can ride alone." His eyes blazed with determination as he turned to the mayor. "You pick."

A nervous laugh skittered from the mayor's lips as he held up his hands. "Now, now, folks, there's no need to blow this out of proportion. You're just sitting on the back of a convertible, passing out candy."

Suddenly, the situation struck Harper as funny. Laughter bubbled in her throat, and she couldn't contain it.

"What's so funny?" Pepper demanded.

Harper shook her head. "This … you." It was astounding the lengths that Pepper would go to in order to ensnare a man. Well, this time the diva was out of luck.

Pepper drew herself up to her full height, her hateful eyes shooting darts at Harper.

Sam gave Harper a concerned look. "Are you okay?"

Harper stepped close to him, linking her arm through his. "Yes, actually, I'm great. You know what? It doesn't matter if you ride in the car with Pepper."

Sam's jaw went slack. "Huh?" He searched her face. "Are you sure?"

"Absolutely." Her eyes locked with his, a burst of tenderness overflowing in her chest for this wonderful, magnificent man who loved her as she loved him. "We've braved a hurricane and murderous criminals, I think we can brave the likes of Pepper McClain too."

Amusement flickered in Sam's jade eyes, and then a grin spread over his lips. "I believe you're right. I love you," he murmured.

"I love you too." Harper touched his cheek and kissed him full on the lips.

"That's the spirit," the mayor said heartily.

Pepper looked like she was about to blow. "You know what? I don't want to ride in the car with you." She lifted her chin in the air and shot Harper a nasty look. "You can have him," she harrumphed as she flounced away.

Harper chuckled. "Thank you, thank you very much," she said in a mock Elvis Presley tone as she winked at Sam. "I'll take him."

Sam just shook his head and laughed. There was a look of admiration on his handsome face. "All right, Dorothy, I'm all yours." He slid an arm around her shoulders and pulled her close. "Do we get to go to Emerald City now?"

She laughed. "You know what they say … 'There's no place like home.'"

His eyes deepened with intensity as his gaze held hers. "The only home I want is a home with you."

That evening, as Harper was getting ready to go on a date with Sam, she got a text from him saying that he'd been called away to a medical emergency at the hospital in Daphne. Swallowing her disappointment, Harper was about to change into a t-shirt and sweats when Andi showed up.

"What're you doing here?" Harper asked as she led Andi into the kitchen. She went to the refrigerator and grabbed a bottle of sparkling water. "Want one?"

"No thanks."

She twisted off the lid and took a long drink, savoring the burn down her throat. "I thought you had a date tonight." She'd closed The Magnolia early to give everyone the night off for the festival.

Andi shrugged. "It got cancelled," she said glumly.

"Mine too. Sam got called in on an emergency at the hospital."

Andi's face brightened. "Hey, I have an idea. Why don't we go to the beach and watch the sunset?"

Harper made a face. "Nah, I think I'll just stick around here and watch a movie."

"Come on," Andi urged, "don't leave me hanging. It's been ages since we've done anything together." She brought her hands together, making a puppy-dog face. "Please?"

Harper sighed. "Okay, you talked me into it. But let me change into something more comfortable first." She looked down at her royal blue blouse and gray slacks.

"You're fine as you are," Andi said impatiently. "Let's just go, or we'll miss the sunset."

Harper rolled her eyes. "All right."

The sun was already starting to go down as Andi drove into the beach district, splashing the sky with strokes of orange and pink. They got out of the car and headed down the boardwalk. When they reached the sand, Harper and Andi kicked off their sandals. Harper breathed in the salty air, appreciating the ocean breeze on her face. "Which direction?"

Andi motioned with her head. "Let's go this way."

They walked in companionable silence a little way up the beach. Up ahead, Harper spotted an elaborate setup with a table and people dressed in formal attire. "Looks like somebody's having a party," she remarked.

As they grew closer, her breath quickened as she sensed something familiar in the posture of the tall figure with broad, confident shoulders. The scene came into shape as she gasped. Standing beside the table was Sam in a white dress shirt and black slacks. There was a white linen tablecloth, set with crystal and china. A bouquet of yellow calla lilies adorned it. Frank, The Magnolia's cook, stood off to the side in his Sunday suit. Harper turned to Andi, who had a cat that ate the canary grin on her face.

Harper stepped up to the table, locking gazes with Sam. "An emergency, huh?"

His eyes sparkled as he grinned. "Are you surprised?"

Harper laughed, a ripple of pleasure running through her. "Yes." She was touched that Sam had gone to all this trouble for her. "This is incredible." There was another table off to the side that held an assortment of covered silver platters. Sam stepped up to her and took her hands. She loved how small her hands were in his. She soaked in his masculinity and rugged features, loving the sparkle of adventure in his vivid green eyes. His eyes deepened, and he seemed to be searching her face. It occurred to her that he was nervous. A second later, he got down on one knee.

Tears misted her eyes as she realized what was happening.

"Harper Boyce," he began, "you're the woman I've been looking for my whole life. I've been literally halfway around the world and never met anyone like you. My life will never be complete unless you're in it." A lopsided grin tugged at his lips. "I was a goner from that first night you made me dinner."

A bubble of joy burst in her chest and spread glowing warmth through her entire body as she laughed. "Ah, now the picture becomes clear. It's my cooking that you love."

Amusement lit his features as he grinned. "You've discovered my weakness."

Fighting a smile, she arched an eyebrow. "Grilled cheese sandwiches?"

He gazed at her with such tenderness that it melted through her like warm butterscotch; smooth, sweet and molten, making her go weak in the knees. In the blink of his eye, she caught a glimpse of the future—a wonderful, glorious future with the man who'd surpassed her wildest dreams … white picket fence and all. "You," he murmured, "it has always been you."

"Yes!" she exclaimed jubilantly.

Sam blinked in surprise.

"He hasn't asked you to marry him yet," Andi piped in with a chuckle.

Harper's eyes rounded, her cheeks growing warm. "Oh."

Sam laughed. "I was working my way around to it. Will you marry me?"

"Yes!" Harper shouted again. "Yes, oh yes!" She fell to her knees and into Sam's arms, laughing and crying at the same time.

Sam stood and helped Harper to her feet. He turned to Andi. "It seems that we have a reception coming up in the near future," he said ceremoniously. "May I officially reserve The Magnolia?"

Wiping her eyes, Andi laughed. "I'll have to ask the owner's approval, but I think it'll work out just fine."

Want more Falling for the Doc romance? Dancing With the Doc is coming soon.

For more romance that takes place in Clementine, Alabama, check out The Hot Headed Patriot (Rigby and Scarlett's story) and The Twelfth Hour Patriot.

YOUR FREE BOOK AWAITS ...

Hey there, thanks for taking the time to read *Cooking With the Doc*. If you enjoyed it, please take a minute to give me a review on Amazon. I really appreciate your feedback, as I depend largely on word of mouth to promote my books.

To receive updates when more of my books are coming out, sign up for my newsletter at:

http://bit.ly/freebookjenniferyoungblood

If you sign up for my newsletter, I'll give you one of my books, Beastly Charm: A contemporary retelling of beauty & the beast, for FREE. Plus, you'll get information on discounts and other freebies. Sign up at:

http://bit.ly/freebookjenniferyoungblood

BOOKS BY JENNIFER YOUNGBLOOD

Billionaire Boss Romance
Her Blue Collar Boss
Her Lost Chance Boss

Georgia Patriots Romance
The Hot Headed Patriot
The Twelfth Hour Patriot
The Unstoppable Patriot

O'Brien Family Romance
The Impossible Groom (Chas O'Brien)
The Twelfth Hour Patriot (McKenna O'Brien)
The Stormy Warrior (Caden O'Brien and Tess Eisenhart)

Christmas
Rewriting Christmas (A Novella)
Yours By Christmas (Park City Firefighter Romance)
Her Crazy Rich Fake Fiancé

Navy SEAL Romance

The Resolved Warrior
The Reckless Warrior
The Diehard Warrior
The Stormy Warrior

The Jane Austen Pact
Seeking Mr. Perfect

Texas Titan Romances
The Hometown Groom
The Persistent Groom
The Ghost Groom
The Jilted Billionaire Groom
The Impossible Groom
The Perfect Catch (Last Play Series)

Hawaii Billionaire Series
Love Him or Lose Him
Love on the Rocks
Love on the Rebound
Love at the Ocean Breeze
Love Changes Everything
Loving the Movie Star
Love Under Fire (A Companion book to the Hawaii Billionaire Series)

Kisses and Commitment Series
How to See With Your Heart

Angel Matchmaker Series
Kisses Over Candlelight
The Cowboy and the Billionaire's Daughter

Romantic Thrillers
False Identity

False Trust
Promise Me Love
Burned

Contemporary Romance
Beastly Charm

Fairytale Retellings (The Grimm Laws Series)
Banish My Heart **(This book is FREE)**
The Magic in Me
Under Your Spell
A Love So True

Southern Romance
Livin' in High Cotton
Recipe for Love
The Secret Song of the Ditch Lilies

Short Stories
The Southern Fried Fix

ABOUT THE AUTHORS

Jennifer loves reading and writing clean romance. She believes that happily ever after is not just for stories. Jennifer enjoys interior design, rollerblading, clogging, jogging, and chocolate. In Jennifer's opinion there are few ills that can't be solved with a warm brownie and scoop of vanilla-bean ice cream.

Jennifer grew up in rural Alabama and loved living in a town where "everybody knows everybody." Her love for writing began as a young teenager when she wrote stories for her high school English teacher to critique.

Jennifer has BA in English and Social Sciences from Brigham Young University where she served as Miss BYU Hawaii in 1989. Before becoming an author, she worked as the owner and editor of a monthly newspaper named *The Senior Times*.

She now lives in the Rocky Mountains with her family and spends her time writing and doing all of the wonderful things that make up the life of a busy wife and mother.

Craig Depew was born in Edmonton, Alberta. His family moved frequently while he was growing each time his dad earned a job promotion. He lived in much of the eastern half of the United States and Canada and after high school lived in Israel, Japan and Grenada. He went to college at BYU and graduated from medical school at Texas Tech. He spent the first half of his medical career outside Atlanta, GA, and then three more years in Statesboro before moving his practice to the Rocky Mountains of Utah, where he continues seeing patients.

In his writing he draws on the places he's lived and visited, people he's known, and news stories that readers will recognize in his work. He began working on his first novel, Missing, Presumed Dead, in 2000 and finished it about three years later. His second novel, Weightless, won Best in Show at the 2013 League of Utah Writers Creative Writing Competition and his third, Transparent, won Honorable Mention in the same contest.

facebook.com/authorjenniferyoungblood

twitter.com/authorjenn1

instagram.com/authorjenniferyoungblood

Made in the USA
Monee, IL
10 February 2021